# FRUIT

# WiLL HERON

A catalogue record for this book is available at the British Library.

ISBN **978-1-7393582-0-4**

Printed in Britain by Biddles, Castle House, PE32 1SF

Cover photography by Hype Photography

Cover design by Rob at Strike Three

will-heron.com

WiLL-HERON.COM

# CONTENTS

A Summer of Fruit.................................................. 1

A Sign of the Times .............................................. 21

Bloody Crusties .................................................... 36

Cream................................................................ 50

Climbing the Ladder ............................................. 65

A Trip to the Country ........................................... 79

Regional Lay-By Manager...................................... 90

Roadworks Everywhere ....................................... 106

Nice Day Off? .................................................... 119

Expansion ......................................................... 130

Wild Horses ...................................................... 146

That Escalated Quickly ....................................... 161

Mr Baguette....................................................... 181

Is that a Helicopter following us?...................................... 205

Big Dog ................................................................. 220

The Sting ................................................................ 230

The End is Nigh.......................................................... 243

# CHAPTER 1

# A SUMMER OF FRUIT

I pulled into the lay-by, avoiding the first pothole and hitting the second, my old car bouncing to a dusty stop. I grabbed my bag and sunglasses and jumped out without thinking, throwing myself back against the car as a huge B&Q juggernaut exploded past me. Taking a few seconds to compose myself, I looked sheepishly up and down the road and headed over to the stall at the side of the lay-by.

"Morning," said the man at the stall. "Strawberries or cherries?"

"No, mate, I'm here to start work. Dave told me to ask for Wilfred."

There was an awkward pause where a reply should have been.

"Are you Wilfred?"

"Yep, you must be Adam," said the now-confirmed Wilfred.

He was about fifty and had seen better days: his belly was significant, and he probably hadn't seen his feet for a good few years. He was a man who clearly enjoyed the questionable health benefits of several bottles of red wine a week and would likely be found tucking into a late-night

Fray Bentos pie. His nose had started to look like he regularly dipped it into a glass of claret as part of some weird wine-tasting technique, it appeared to be slowly turning into a beef knuckle which had been chewed by an enthusiastic dog.

"Dave said I should show you the ropes, and then I can finally go on me holiday," he complained.

"Well, how hard can it be?" I said foolishly.

"Don't get me started, Adam; how hard can it fucking be... Harder than you think, son, that's how fucking hard."

I'd triggered him, and he proceeded to take me down a twenty-minute rabbit hole of complaints, largely consisting of slightly dubious descriptions of his customers. The comments were mixed with short snippets of useful information about the job and all that could go wrong in the allegedly complex world of fruit selling. He ranted about 'coachloads of bloody Orientals coming over here to take fucking photos of everything', then dropped in casually that I should always get the money first. Then off he zoomed about Brummies all being idiots and never trusting anyone with an accent (all said with a slight South West twang), followed by some tips on keeping the fruit fresh with a cool box. He then offered a final dive into his thoughts on Londoners, or "Cockney Twats" as he called them, and how they were all cunts.

Just when it felt like his spiel might go on forever, it ended abruptly.

"Well, that's it, change is in there. I'm off on me hols."

Before I could blink, Wilfred, moving fast for a man of

his belly, was gone, leaving only a cloud of dust and a lingering smell of Brut in his place.

I sat down, had a look in the money belt, ate a cherry and lit a slightly wrinkled old spliff end I found by surprise in my cigarette pack. I waited for the first customer; perhaps this would be a nice quiet job, and I could just sit in the sun all day relaxing. The view across the rolling hills was certainly dramatic, although the constant noise of the road wasn't particularly adding to the ambience. I'd only been back in the country for a month or so, and the consensus was that I should get a real job and "sort my life out" – two things I'd never been great at. But I'd put my friends and family through a lot in the last few years, so I figured I could at least give it a go. I didn't feel up to going full cyborg and getting an office job, so I thought maybe I'd ease myself into my new way of life with some fruit-selling in the sun. I pictured myself eating strawberries all day and having occasional chats with people about how fresh they were. So far so good I thought, munching a strawberry.

A VW campervan juddered to a halt in front of me; it was bright green and had an ironic wobbly Hawaiian dancer on the dashboard and some plastic-looking, no doubt also ironic, flowers around the windscreen. Two super-hipster Londoners jumped out, both wearing thick-rimmed black glasses. He had a moustache borrowed from a French heroin dealer in the 70s; hers was more subtle. She wore rockabilly dungarees and a vintage bow in her hair; he wore corduroy trousers and a bright yellow varsity jacket. They couldn't have looked more out of place if they'd tried.

"Look, they are totally real. I told you it was a thing," she said to him.

"Strawberries or cherries?" I offered.

"Too much, bro, it's too much," he said.

"They're only £2.50. How much are they in London?"

This seemed to confuse him for a second. He'd never considered that people might be able to tell where he was from just by looking at him. He looked like a man who, if he said he was going up north, meant Camden and not Newcastle.

"Man, not the p. £2.50 is a deal, a *steal*. It's too much that you sit here all day selling fruit."

"Do you want any strawberries, or have you just popped by to make me feel good about my life choices? I only started doing this an hour ago."

He burst out laughing. She gave him a look.

"Can we have two punnets of strawberries, please?" she said, holding out a twenty.

I took the cash and passed the fruit over with her change.

"Sorry about him, his family have got a house in Cornwall." She looked embarrassed by both the moron she had come away with and the reason she'd come away with him.

"Sorry to hear that," I said.

They jumped back into the camper with him asking her, "What's wrong, babe?" about fifteen times on the way. Off they sped in a cloud of Shoreditch dust, leaving only the faintest waft of ironically worn Old Spice behind.

That was just the first customer in what would be a longer and far less relaxing day than I had previously imagined. But as the customers kept coming, I realised that maybe I would be so busy that I wouldn't get distracted or bored. Perhaps that was always the problem with my previous attempts at a normal life.

After university, I'd given normality a stab. I managed to land a job as the manager of a small local Co-Op – honestly, I think they were just desperate to get some graduates into their company, which was, by all accounts, mostly managed by a selection of life's more terrifying mutants.

Still, I got so bored with the day-to-day mundanity of it all. I was going out of my mind, the place was empty half the time and the customers were all that kept me from quitting each day. They were an odd and amusing bunch; so odd that when someone came in to rob the shop at gunpoint, I thought they were joking. I kept asking him if this was some kind of weird head office joke (they were a strange bunch in the Co-Op head office). He kept waving a gun in my face and telling me to give him the money. I think he was new to the whole robbery thing and my attitude wasn't helping. After about five minutes I realised he was real, so I pressed the silent alarm button while I got him £40 from the till. He didn't look happy with this. I explained that most people used cards these days. It looked like this hadn't occurred to him. He ran away after grabbing a handful of chewing gum, more out of frustration than any desire to have fresh breath.

As I watched him run down the street, he tripped and

smashed his teeth out on the side of the pavement. I considered going to check if he was OK. Seconds later, a police car pulled up in front of him and that was the end of that sad saga. Weirdly head office didn't see the funny side of me thinking it was a prank they'd arranged, and I was fired the next day.

Keeping myself busy selling fruit, might well be my saviour; by midday, I'd taken nearly a grand. A seemingly endless queue of people, desperate to get out of the car just to break the monotony of their drive, were my new customers. This must be why motorway services are so popular, despite being as expensive as an airport terminal and almost as awful.

My first coach of the day pulled up. It was a large group of Asian tourists. A young man in a uniform came out quietly onto the lay-by and looked over towards me. I waved, and he walked over.

"Strawberries or cherries?"

"Sorry, my English isn't perfect," said the young Chinese man in near-perfect English.

"That's OK. Would you like strawberries," I said, waving towards a large pile of strawberry punnets on the left, "or cherries?" I gestured to the right.

"Yes."

"OK, how many?"

"Yes."

"How many?"

"Yes, please, all of them."

"All of them?"

"Yes, all of the fruit, please. How much?"

I counted all the punnets on the table. It seemed like about £250, rounding it up to £280. I told him the price and expected him to object.

Instead, he said, "OK, thank you," and passed over a pile of crisp ten-pound notes. He then opened up a large bag which he unfolded from nowhere.

I loaded the punnets into the bag for him, and with a quick thank you and another apology for his bad (perfect) English, off he popped back to the coach full of very excited-looking tourists. As they drove off, I could see them politely ripping the bag apart and spraying weird sachets of sauce onto the strawberries.

I loaded the rest of my fruit onto the stall and dealt with another hour of non-stop cockneys. Were they migrating en masse?

A massive and slightly yellowing caravan wobbled to a halt with an old Vauxhall estate towing it. Out jumped two very red-faced Northern caravaners; you could spot them from a mile off, their red-faced gammon glow and meat-eating gout limp always a giveaway. They were also, very noticeably, never ever happy.

"These aren't as good as the Yorkshire cherries, are they, Elaine?"

"Oh no, Nigel, they aren't at that. You can't beat a good Yorkshire cherry, can you?"

*You should have brought some with you, you massive twat.*

Everyone else would jump straight back in their car, coach, or camper, happy that the awkward transaction was over. But not our Nigel and Elaine. They wanted to make you suffer. They'd stand there slowly testing and evaluating every cherry and strawberry, assessing how it compared to the staggering beauty and explosive perfection of fruit from Yorkshire. Mine were far inferior to the Yorkshire version, of course, no doubt due to the superiority of the Yorkshire sun, the Yorkshire water, and the Yorkshire manure. The last of which seemed particularly prevalent as it poured out of them the moment they opened their mouths.

"We're off to a campsite in Devon," Elaine tells me.

"We went to Northern France last year," Nigel butts in.

"Small puddings?" I asked.

On a few visits to France, I'd learned that Yorkshire folk were never happy with the size of French desserts.

"Fucking small puddings, not like in Yorkshire. If you're going to charge six quid for a pudding, it needs to be a big pudding, and they bring out this tiny little pudding. Well, I said to Elaine, I'm not happy!"

"He did. He said he wasn't happy to the waiter."

"I told him, I'm not fucking happy, *garçon*. This pudding is fucking tiny."

"I bet you did, mate. What do the French know about desserts, anyway?"

"Exactly. Have you been?" He was happy to have maybe found another pudding revolutionary brother-in-arms.

"Que savent les français des desserts."

He looked startled, as if I'd pulled a rabbit out of his wife's ear.

"Oh, sorry, I didn't realise you were foreign. I'm just trying to relax on my holiday."

"That's alright, mate. Don't panic. I'm English."

He looked baffled. His wife started pulling him towards the caravan. Her face looked horrified. They'd shared their deepest dessert desires with someone foreign. Oh, the shame if they find out about this back home.

"Come on, Nigel, let's go. We want to get a good spot for the caravan," she said, backing away.

They couldn't get out of there quickly enough. Success, I thought. I've found these people's Achilles heel. I just had to talk to them in French, and off they scuttle.

No wonder the French hate us. I'm sure there are more complicated historical reasons, but Nigel and Elaine weren't helping matters.

A dirty blue people carrier pulled up in the lay-by a few minutes later, with their speakerphone on through the stereo. It was on too loud, and I could hear every word of their conversation.

"I've got to go, Mum; he's going to piss himself in a minute."

A whirlwind of family chaos descended onto the potholed tarmac. The mum, who had been on the phone, jumped out with a slightly terrifying 'I've had eight too many coffees' look on her face. The dad slowly clambered out of the passenger side. He had a pre-beer thousand-yard stare normally reserved for people who'd served in Nam.

*You weren't there, man. You don't know. I can still hear the screams.*

His private Vietnam was just the drudgery of a marriage that had long since lost its spark and some

9

children that he never wanted, who screamed a lot. They also mysteriously looked like his best friend, Darren.

The screaming child was extracted from the back of the car by the now-frantic mum. She rushed him over to the side of the lay-by and held him at arm's length over a patch of stinging nettles. He pissed everywhere; he had a bright future as a fountain ahead of him. After he'd finished watering the entire hedge, she physically shook him up and down and then plonked him down on the ground. You could almost see a wave of relaxed vibes waft through her as he stopped screaming, pissing and needing a piss all at once.

She looked around and accidentally made eye contact with me.

"Strawberries?" I said the moment eye contact was made.

She looked super-guilty about what had just happened; she glanced over at her husband. He was smoking a cigarette and staring obliviously over the fields. No doubt, thinking about how his life used to be before little Timmy the fountain turned up one day unannounced. These wistful thoughts probably included beer and football, and football and beer. But still, any memory, no matter how tediously stereotypical, was a welcome change from the weekend of hell he was no doubt heading into. She realised he was going to be no help.

"Er, two strawberries, please," she hesitantly suggested, more out of embarrassment than anything. As if the lay-by was some kind of pay-per-use toilet that handily came with free fruit, and I was its keeper. Maybe I should set up a table with some cheap bottles of aftershave and a silver change dish for donations.

I passed her the strawberries, and she handed me the exact change.

"Sorry," she muttered, "he just desperately needed a wee."

"Weeeeeeee," Timmy screamed.

"When you've got to go, you've got to go."

She dragged Timmy back to the car. They'd have still bought a punnet or two if they'd all been fruit-intolerant.

At the end of day one, I felt bored, tired and dirty all the same time. I'd taken £1640. That didn't seem too shabby, but I had nothing to measure it against. I text the boss, Dave, my total and how many punnets were left for the day. He was a stocky, well-built chap in his early fifties with dark, swept-back hair and a well-travelled face. He was chatty without being in any way friendly. He had eyes that looked like they had witnessed dark and terrible things. I hadn't quite figured him out yet, but I imagined he'd be pleased to know that I'd smashed nearly two grand on my first day. I loaded the small table and chairs into my car, along with the last few punnets of fruit.

Dave text me back, *Well done. I'll move my retirement forward a day.*

I imagined wrong, clearly. I hadn't taken him for a sarky twat. Better than a moody arsehole, though, I guess. I jumped in my car and sped off for home; luckily, I only lived fifteen minutes away. I couldn't wait to wash the petrol fumes off me, not to mention the fruit goo, which had somehow got everywhere. I could feel my love of strawberries slipping away already. They would forever be linked to the stench of petrol and roadside grime.

My house already had a slightly strange waft to it. I'd inherited it before I moved back to England and hadn't yet had the time or the inclination to make it my own. It was kitted out with furniture from the early 90s – not quite old enough to be retro chic, and not new enough to be achingly on-trend. My living room consisted of a sofa, an armchair and a TV stand. The sofa was a charming faded off-cream colour. It was comfortable, though, which was a plus. The armchair had one of those greasy spots where the back of a head had left a mark after a decade of nice sit-downs. I tended to avoid it. The walls were thankfully painted white, a small mercy as the bedroom was painted bright red. If Laurence Llewelyn-Bowen passionately hated you, he would paint your bedroom in this shade of red.

I jumped in the shower, ignoring the bathroom's cheeky plastic laminate floor with peeling corners. Perhaps it would magically fix itself. I wasn't the best at DIY. I had tried to put some shelves up in the kitchen a few weeks before, but after several holes, three trips to B&Q to get the right drill bits, and one visit from the odd-job man to fix my disaster, I made a conscious decision not to do any more DIY ever again. I showered and slept on the sofa, afraid of going anywhere near the bedroom's red paint.

The following day, I headed to the warehouse to collect the fresh fruit for the day and drop off the previous day's takings. When I arrived, the large fenced-in forecourt was full of old men. It looked like the smoking area of a bingo hall. A group of sixty to seventy-year-old gents stood around nattering about caravans and their wives, blowing steam off cups of tea while they did so. They loved them passionately and spent all their wages on them; a few of them were fond of their wives too.

I walked onto the forecourt. The large warehouse loomed in front of me like a metal goliath. It probably looked very futuristic in the 90s when they built it. It was entirely made of metal with blue horizontal cladding covering all but the roof. It had faded from its once crisp colour into a dirty washed-out dark blue. Two large metal doors were opened outwards onto the courtyard. Inside I could glimpse tables covered in packages and people busily putting fruit into punnets. I avoided talking to anyone and quickly grabbed the day's fruit allocation. These people were too much for me at this time of day, possibly at any time of day.

I arrived, set up my little pitch and poured myself a coffee out of my super stylish He-Man thermos flask. The sun was shining, and it was quiet before the morning rush hour. I sat, lit a slightly naughty morning spliff and sipped my coffee, looking out over the picturesque green hillside. A light mist rolled in on the breeze over the hills towards me, and a flock of geese flew out of the mist like low-level bombers. I heard a car pull up and some heavy footsteps heading my way.

"Hi there, how are you this fine morning?" bellowed an impossibly loud American accent from an impossibly loud American man in his fifties.

Jesus, it's too early for this, I thought as I quickly put out the spliff.

"Hi. I wonder if you can help us, we're lost. Which way is Stonehenge? I think we missed it."

Americans were always disappointed by how small Stonehenge was, how close to the road it was and how few druids there seemed to be lurking around doing weird shit with mushrooms and herbs. I wondered where their expectations came from. It seemed like they expected something akin to the pyramids architecturally, manned with troops of dancing maidens and long-bearded druids burning sage. Perhaps they thought it was something to do with King Arthur and Merlin. You could almost taste their disappointment. Wait until they saw the rest of our once allegedly Great Britain. The only good things we had left were largely disappointing ruins.

"About twenty miles back the way you just came."

"Thanks so much. It's just so adorable around here," his quite frankly terrifying wife said. She'd escaped the confines of the hot car to get involved in the conversation. She looked like she'd just stepped off the set of a low-budget Italian mafia film. She was all big jewellery, massive hair and long, pointy nails.

"And what do you do?"

"I sell strawberries and cherries. Would you like some?"

"How quaint, Tony, ain't that cutest thing you ever saw? Let's buy some," she squawked.

"Two punnets for a fiver?"

"Sure, which one is that?"

I took the twenty-pound note from her and handed her back a pound coin, just to confuse things. I quickly passed her over two punnets of fruit before she noticed.

"Thanks again, mate," he said like an extra from *Chitty Chitty Bang Bang*.

Thankfully, my sarcasm chip hadn't kicked in today, and it barely registered.

"No problem, enjoy the stones. Say hi to the chief druid, and don't forget – don't look him in the eyes."

He looked excited and confused by this thought as he waddled back to his car.

The morning drifted along; car fumes bellowed, people stopped, people didn't, and on it rolled. The sunshine beat down, and my children's thermos flask was running dry already. The baking sunshine wasn't making the sticky fruit smell any more delightful. I tried to keep all the punnets out of the sun. The strawberries were worse than the cherries. The sticky smell was starting to permeate my skin, and my constant bored nibbling of one from each punnet wasn't helping.

An old-school Land Rover pulled up. Not my usual customer's vehicle of choice. It was a proper off-roader, with one of those snorkel devices attached to the side, for people who liked to take their cars for a swim. Two farm types with beards jumped out and headed over. One wore an old tweed jacket he barely fitted into, while the other younger one had a scar down his cheek and a mullet hanging down his vested back. He looked like he dated his cousin and his sister was getting jealous.

"Strawberries or cherries?" I offered in a slightly

embarrassed tone, feeling that this was unlikely to be why they were here.

"Two strawberries," the older one grunted, much to my surprise.

This felt weird; he didn't seem like a strawberry-eater and even less like a strawberry-buyer. I would have thought he was more at home in the queue for a steak and mushroom pie. Perhaps he was trying to get his one a day.

"Five pounds, please."

He pulled out a leather wallet and plucked a fifty out from its cosy position nestled between its many similar-looking friends.

"Can you *break* this?" the emphasis was on break.

"Sure, no problem," I said, trying to keep it light.

I pulled my money belt out and took his fifty. I tucked it into the open money belt and pulled him out his change.

"That's a lot of money to be sitting out here with all by yourself."

"Yeah, a lot of money," his previously silent and thoroughly inbred friend interjected.

*What the fuck is going on here? I feel like I'm about to be mugged by some off-roading farmers with a taste for strawberries.*

"It's been a busy day," I responded, hoping this wasn't about to go in the direction it felt like it might.

He grabbed the two punnets of fruit out of my hands and took a big angry bite out of a massive strawberry, tossing the remaining half at my feet.

"A lot of money, lot of moneyyyyyyyy." He slowed himself down at the end like a record deck that had been unplugged.

They looked at each other and laughed like a pair of old pirates. Spinning around, they left as quickly as they had arrived, leaving behind a cloud of dust and a waft of Lynx Africa and manure.

I figured I'd keep this strange interaction to myself. I didn't want them to think I attracted trouble or sack me for being a pain in the arse in my first week. I'd already been told to 'fuck off' when I asked where I was meant to go for a piss and how long my lunch break was. Spoiler alert, in the field and in between customers, seemed to be the answers. But I'm sure Dave probably didn't have any interest in me feeling intimidated by a pair of fruit-loving farmers. They did pay, after all.

I'd noticed from my last few morning warehouse stop-offs that perhaps he was slightly more intimidating than I had first given him credit for. I'd heard a few of the older lay-by workers chatting nervously about him. Perhaps after spending most of my adult life around the fringes of normal society, my perspective of friendly and normal had become slightly skewed.

The rest of the afternoon zoomed past. Fortunately, I was way too busy to notice how boring this job was. I had a rare five minutes with no customers, so thought I'd have a sneaky fag and a coffee. As always in life, the moment I sat back and relaxed for a second, a car pulled up.

"Alright mate, can I grab some strawberries?"

I walked over to the stall to oblige.

"Adam?"

I looked up at the customer. It took me a couple of seconds to work out that it was someone I went to school with. I couldn't quite place his name.

"It's Alfie," he said, sensing my hesitation.

"Sorry, oh yeah shit, Alfie. How are you? I haven't seen you since just after we finished school." To be precise, I'd seen him a couple of times since then. But he hadn't seen me, and I'd changed directions or scooted off down an alleyway. He was nice enough, I just couldn't handle anyone from my school days. I tried to put it as far behind me as possible. There were always too many questions.

"What you been up to?" he asked. He seemed genuinely happy to see me.

"This and that. I've just come back from Spain a little while ago, so I thought I'd enjoy the sunshine and earn some cash."

"Fair enough, mate, why the fuck not."

"What about you?"

"Working in my old man's car showroom still. Same old shit."

"I'd nearly forgotten about that place. How's your dad?"

His old man ran a second-hand car dealership on the edge of town. We used to earn a few quid pocket money cleaning the cars for him on the weekends when I was about ten.

"He's good, mate, same old. How's your mum?"

The question I was dreading! I could sense its arrival; it was like a guided scud missile, one I could see coming but never stop.

"She passed away, mate. About a year after my old man."

His face changed, as everyone's always did.

"Shit Adam, I'm so sorry mate, your mum was great. So sorry."

I passed him over a couple of punnets of strawberries.

"On the house, Alfie. It was nice to see you." I offered him an out, and like almost all English men talking about grief, he took it. I couldn't blame him. I wanted out too.

"Thanks. See you around," he said, getting back in his car.

This was the reason I avoided people from my school. They all loved my mum; they always asked after her and then I always looked like I'd ruined their week. I was the harbinger of bad tidings and bleakness.

Within seconds I had a queue again and had to tuck the feelings away back where they liked to hide. I had to call for a refill around 1pm as I was all out of strawberries. Twenty minutes later, a young Polish guy in a white van with Tina Turner blaring out pulled up. He unloaded a pile of boxes from the back and brought them over. He had a super retro Kappa matching tracksuit on, was about six foot something and was sporting a kind of Eminem blond skinhead.

"Reload?" he said as he dumped them down. "Busy today?"

"Yeah, it's been non-stop."

"Good, good, boss says to keep up good work," he shouted over Tina Turner. "I am Gregg, with two g's." He shook me firmly by the hand.

"Greg always has two g's," I said, confused.

"Gregg. G.R.E.G.G. Two g's."

"Nice to meet you, Gregg, with two g's."

He jumped back in his van, screeching off with a wave, nearly hitting a busload of tourists looking for Stonehenge. Five minutes later, they had turned around and pulled over for some cherries and directions.

Another £700 later, and I called it a day.

£1733! I texted the boss the total and started packing up. I vaguely expected at least a well-done, perhaps a bonus – honestly, even a smiley face would have done.

*Where the fuck did the £3 come from. They are £2.50 each. You don't need to text me the total every fucking day*, was what I got in response. How much fruit can one man sell in a day? More than £1733 was clearly required to generate some vague enthusiasm.

I packed up and set off for home, exhausted and stinking of petrol and fruit once again.

# CHAPTER 2

# A SIGN OF THE TIMES

I was up early the next day. On waking, I had a strong urge for a full English; I hadn't had one for years, and today was the day.

I parked and walked past some unfamiliar-looking hipster coffee shops to my favourite old greasy spoon. It hadn't changed a bit; if anything, it looked even more dated than I'd remembered. Old greasy framed pictures on the wall, a chalkboard crookedly on the wall above the counter, with endless variations of breakfasts that should carry a health warning. I went for the "Big Breakfast Special", deciding to swerve the "Gut Buster" with the same misguided enthusiasm as people who order a Diet Coke with their McDonalds.

Minutes later, the culinary delights of our proud flag-waving nation were plonked on the plastic tablecloth in front of me. Fried bread, toast, bacon, two sausages, a hash brown, baked beans, two fried eggs and a few chips. After a few mouthfuls of flabby bacon and microwaved beans, my enthusiasm was waning. I took a bite of a piece of fried bread; the oil oozed into my mouth. That was it for me – the food hadn't changed, but maybe my taste had. I pushed my plate to one side, took a sip from a truly awful mug of coffee and left disappointed.

Well, that was a total waste of time and taste buds I thought while driving towards the lay-by. It didn't take me long to get there, as the roads were weirdly empty. As I got close I could see black smoke wisping up into the air ahead. A few seconds later, I drove past a smouldering 'Cherries at next lay-by' sign. Well, that can't be good. I slowed down for the next one as the smoke seemed thicker. It was still on fire; a poorly hand-drawn strawberry was burning brightly.

I drove slowly past the burning sign and pulled into the lay-by. I walked down to the far end to check the other signs, crossing the road to get a better look. I could see two thin trails of smoke. Little fuckers, they'd done all of them. Who does something like that? Got to be kids. It's staggering the lengths people will go to for entertainment.

I went to my car, got a bottle of water out of the back, and headed over to the burning strawberry. It was nearly burned out by the time I arrived; I poured the whole bottle over the sign until it was just a smoking black mess. I gave it a quick but careful stamp to make sure it was all out and wasn't going to blow all over the road.

I went back to the car to see if I had any more water. Instead, I found an old bottle of Coke and an ancient bottle of Fanta. I guess they'd have to do. I set off to the first sign I'd seen, narrowly avoiding some very angry-sounding lorries honking their horns. I poured the Fanta over the smouldering sign, and a plume of sweet and sickly black smoke headed straight up my nose.

I gagged and thought I was going to throw up. I bent over with my hands on my knees, looking at the ground. I took a few seconds and then stood up, feeling slightly better. As I did, a Land Rover slowed down as it approached me. I thought maybe it was because I looked like I was about to vomit everywhere. People will rubberneck at anything. I looked up at them as they passed. I recognised the two farm weirdos from the other day. Hard to forget those two. They looked right at me as they drove past very slowly, like in an Aphex Twin video, both cackling like drunk seamen.

Heading back to the two signs at the other end of the lay-by, I wondered if this was the kind of thing I should call the police about. I could just imagine how perfectly the call would go. *Yes, certainly, we'll get a couple of cars and a forensic squad straight out.* The police could barely be bothered to help if there was a genuine emergency these days, let alone come out for smouldering fruit signs. I'd be in for a long wait, I suspected.

I poured the Coke over the next two signs and gave them a good stamp; the Coke conjured a sickly smoke smell that tasted like death.

I thought I'd better call the boss. I dialled, and he picked up far too quickly as if he was waiting for me.

"What's going on?" he snapped down the phone.

"Someone set fire to all the signs?"

"Fuck's sake, get your arse down to the warehouse."

He sounded far from happy with my news. Not my fault, though. I jumped in the car and sped off to the warehouse. I'd yet to make it inside – I loaded up my car out the front each morning, and my interview had been in the car park. Dave pretty much just checked I was from Earth and that I had a car. He barely glanced at my C.V. nor stopped to interrogate its lies, and the job was mine. I guessed I was overqualified for selling fruit. Half the other sellers I'd seen were over the age of sixty and doing a bit of summer work to pay for some crap for their caravan.

I was coming up to another pitch with just such a chap. He was called Arthur, and he liked caravans and the north of France. He talked of nothing else. I approached a now familiar scene – two smouldering signs and a very stressed-out-looking Arthur on the phone. I didn't stop; he looked like he had the situation in hand, and I couldn't bear to hear about his fucking caravan.

I drove past his lay-by and passed another two signs smoking by the side of the road. It must have been those fucking farmy weirdos in the Land Rover.

I pulled into the industrial estate. The 'New Water Business Park' being once new and nowhere near any water. It looked like every other anonymous English business park, with some trees vaguely pretending to hide the enormous hideous warehouses behind them and a stream of children in cars heading to the new "Soft Play Adventure Land". Business parks were no longer just the home of endless unknown brands making things you'd never heard of; now they were entertainment destinations for desperate mums, dying to get a few moments of peace from their hectic lives. They dumped their kids into a gigantic, dirty cesspit of plastic balls, hoping they might vanish forever through an interdimensional wormhole at the bottom of the ball pit, while they enjoyed a coffee and a catch-up with the other mums.

Luckily, the fruit warehouse was at the other end of the estate. I turned onto the road it was on, the giant front doors were open, and a very unhappy-looking Dave stood in the middle on his phone. He looked stressed and was shouting at someone as I pulled up and parked. His face was flushed red, and I could see the vein on the side of his head throbbing from inside my car.

"I don't fucking get it. I just don't fucking get why you'd do that?"

He hung up and trained his laser-beam stare on me.

"You didn't call the police, did you Adam?"

"No! I can't imagine they'd help much with this kind of thing."

"Try telling fucking Arthur that, fucking caravan-dwelling twat. Anyway, get in the office." He turned and stomped into the warehouse, waving me to follow him from over his shoulder.

The inside of the warehouse, which I'd only glimpsed at before, was an industrially daring bare metal wall look with charming grey cement floors. It was filled with rows of large white tables with people sitting behind them. They were cutting open plastic Sainsbury's containers of strawberries and emptying them into the punnets we sold. Enormous stacks of punnets were everywhere, as were huge sacks of plastic containers spilling out all over the floor. There were little red splotches of squashed fruit all over the place, like giant squatted mosquitos.

At the end of the main room, in the middle, was a

25

metal staircase, which we headed up and went straight into an office that overlooked the warehouse floor. Two men were sat in armchairs, both drinking espressos from tiny glasses.

"This is Terry and Hans the German," said Dave pointing at them. They both nodded and carried on chatting over their coffees. Hans didn't seem to object to being called 'the German' even though it seemed a bit old school to me – but then I don't suppose they got the political correctness memo. Maybe if he'd said "English Terry and Hans the German" it would have seemed less off. Terry looked like he'd quite like to be called English Terry, or British Terry, or maybe even Anglo-Saxon Terry.

Dave made himself an espresso from a very expensive-looking machine and sat down with an audible groan behind a large desk. An offer of a coffee for me wasn't forthcoming.

"What happened then? I'm all fucking ears."

I told him exactly what had happened, and he quietly listened, slurping his coffee loudly and nodding. I told him about the weird, beardy men and their visit the day before.

"Well, you did the right thing, good lad. I'm pretty sure I know one of the cunts you're talking about. They're that Cornish lot that we had trouble with a couple of years ago. Call themselves The Swashbucklers or something tragic like that."

"Fucking pirates again," moaned Terry, "for God's sake."

"Pirates?" chirped Hans in a thick German accent.

"It was the year before you started, Hans," said Dave.

"They came down mob-handed one year and tried to take over half our lay-bys. They did the same thing all the way up to the North Devon area. Making a land grab for the whole South West."

"Cheeky fuckers," muttered Terry.

"Terry gave that big dumb fucker his scar, if I remember rightly."

"I did. Fucking prick pissed on my leg. Pissed on my actual leg. Fucking unbelievable."

"He pissed on you?" I asked. "How?"

"He took his fucking stupid, Cornish cock out and started pissing," laughed Dave.

Even Hans cracked a smile. Terry didn't look overly happy with the trip down memory lane.

"But did you not see him take his penis out?" asked a curious Hans.

"No, I fucking didn't, you prick. His fucking mate distracted me. The first thing I knew about it was a warm feeling on my leg."

Everyone laughed.

"Well, I fucking cut the little twat; he wasn't so cocky then, was he," said an angry Terry. "He was lucky I didn't cut his prick off."

"Joking aside," snapped Dave, "we'll have to be on the watch for them."

"Yeah, we're on it," said Terry and whispered something to Hans, who jumped up, finished his coffee and left without a word.

"Adam, go with Terry, he'll sort you out some new signs and give you a hand putting them up," said Dave, waving us towards the door.

That was that. Problem solved. Terry got up and put on an old-school sheepskin jacket. He was bigger than he looked when I came in. He had a massive pair of sideburns and a skinhead – a slightly weird combination, admittedly, but it seemed to be working for him. He looked like the middle-aged love child of Wolverine and that guy from *Minder*.

"Come on then," he growled at me as he headed out of the office and down the stairs.

We went through the warehouse to the front and around to a side alley. There was a pile of signs, wooden steaks, and a few hammers. The signs looked like the experimental ones that had gone slightly wrong. How do you spell strawberries? I'm sure there are more Rs than that. Minor details, I guess.

"Grab a couple of those," Terry ordered, pointing at the signs. He picked up some stakes and a hammer, like an 80s vampire hitman tooling up. I grabbed an armful of signs, and we headed back to the front of the warehouse. We loaded it all into a slightly battered black Range Rover. He slammed the boot shut and told me to leave my piece of shit car here but grab everything I needed. I nodded more politely than I wanted to. I grabbed the fruit and stall out of the back of my car and put it on his back seat, and jumped in.

We drove out of the estate, past endless white vans and warehouses full of people doing business and along the roads the way I'd come in. Past Arthur, who was now sitting in his car looking like he was possibly crying while on the phone.

"Probably his wife," I said.

"She's a bit of a terror," Terry said. "Have you met her?"

"No, I've only met him a few quick times in passing."

"I went round his house last year to drop his wages off and got stuck with her in the front garden for about an hour. She's a fucking monster," he laughed. "She was going on about how his wages were late, and it wasn't acceptable, and why couldn't he have next week off. They wanted to go and see her sister. I couldn't get a word in. I couldn't escape. She just kept complaining. Then he came out, and it got even worse. She started giving it the big-un. 'Arthur; you tell them what you said to me. Tell them about how much sun cream you use. Go on, tell them.' I had to tell her to shut the fuck up in the end."

"How did that go down?" I wondered out loud.

"Not fucking well," said Terry as we pulled into my lay-by. He jumped out of his Range Rover. "Set the shit up, and I'll get these fucking signs sorted."

"No problem."

I started to unload everything while Terry pulled a sign, a stake and a hammer out of his car. He strode purposefully towards the far end of the lay-by. As I unfolded the chair and piled up punnets of fruit on the table, I could hear swearing and hammering in between the noise of occasional lorries. By the time he was done knocking seven shades of shit out of a wooden stake at the far end, I had a queue. It must have been the sight of Terry carrying out the live installation that was drawing them in. Nothing like the site of a red-faced skinhead with enormous pork chops hitting something with a hammer by the side of the road to make you want a cherry.

I had three posh Chelsea Londoners telling me how quintessentially British my fruit was when Terry walked back. He overheard them as he approached, and I could almost see the anger flowing out of him – he started changing colour, and there may have been steam emanating from his ears. He took two steps towards Toby, the chinless Eton twat who was standing furthest away from me. He was nibbling one of the strawberries he had just bought and looked like he might choke on it through his stifled laughter. Terry's hammer appeared from nowhere, smashing the punnet of strawberries out of Toby's hand and into the field.

"Fuck off," he snarled at them.

They scurried back to their Tesla quicker than Elon Musk with a rocket up his arse.

"Fucking cockney toffs," shouted Terry, waving his hammer at them as they sped off down the road. His hatred for people seemed to have no social positioning; he hated everyone equally.

"At least they bought something; sometimes, they just seem to come and take the piss while they stretch their legs."

"Liberty. Don't know how you guys do it. I wouldn't last ten minutes out here without an incident."

"What kind of incident?" I asked.

"You know, just an incident," he said as he grabbed another two signs and stakes from his car and walked off towards the other burned-out signs. Two screaming children ran over to buy some cherries. I could hear swearing and hammering again; I hoped nobody noticed.

"Cherries or strawberries?" I asked.

"Two cherries, please," said the small boy.

"Mummy, mummy," said the girl. "What's a twatting sign?"

Mummy didn't look overly impressed with Terry's efforts to erect a sign, seemingly using bad language and his fist.

"It's just a special type of sign. Now give the nice man the money." She passed over a five-pound note and skipped her way back to the car. The mum didn't skip and gave me a look like she wanted to hit me with one of the signs.

Terry appeared out of the hedge a few minutes later, brandishing a hammer with a glint in his eye.

"I'm off; here's my mobile number; any more problems, call me. I'll be around this area all day, and I'll pick you up at the end."

He jumped in his Range Rover and was off. That was all the customer interaction he could handle for the day.

Well, that was eventful. I sat down, poured myself a coffee, and lit a much-needed herbal cigarette. I'd upgraded my flask to a grown-up one; it was black and had a cup on the top. A step up from He-Man! I guess I hadn't had much use for a thermos flask since I was into He-Man. I still had a lot of time for Skeletor. But He-Man seemed like a bit of a cock now that I was older. Was He-Man even still a thing? Maybe it was worth a fortune on the ironic crap market. I should probably fish it out of the bin.

A group of Japanese tourists appeared; I was miles away, staring across the field, thinking about 80s cartoons and enjoying some fruity green. I hadn't noticed the coach pull up.

"Two strawberries, please."

I jumped up and passed them over. Well, that was less than normal, I thought. Normally they buy a load for the whole bus. With that thought, a seemingly endless stream of tourists, largely in hilarious hats, headed off the coach and in my direction.

Thirty minutes, thirty-five punnets of strawberries and fifteen photos of me with people I didn't know later, and they were gone. Definitely easier when one person buys them all; maybe it should be a rule. For health and safety reasons or some similar nonsense. Perhaps a sign in different languages was called for. I'm not sure I could handle that ten times a day. I didn't fancy hundreds of pictures of me floating around the internet every day – not the anonymous life I was hoping for.

The day whirled by in an endless succession of coaches of tourists, mostly from Japan and China, with one party from Taiwan. All of them were fantastically polite and friendly. Almost all of them were armed with cameras and some form of excessive headwear. They were a happy bunch compared to all the others who passed by. They seemed to be having a genuinely fantastic time, and that was just my experience of them in a lay-by buying smoke-covered fruit. Imagine how happy they'd be at an actual tourist attraction. They must have been shitting rainbows. Although with the number of coaches today, I was beginning to suspect that there was a strange Chinese website which listed fruit buying in lay-bys as one of the authentic British traditions to try on your holiday. Halfway down the list, somewhere in between watching lunatics chasing a cheese down a near-vertical hill and enjoying the slightly xenophobic merits of a troupe of Morris dancers in the car park of a once charming pub.

I sold my last punnet of cherries and decided to pack up for the day and wait for Terry. I could already feel myself getting bored of the daily monotony of this job, and I'd hardly been at it for long. The tragic realisation that I couldn't even manage to stick at a job selling fruit at the side of the road was interrupted by Terry's arrival. He popped the boot open while he chatted on the phone. I guess I was loading everything up then. I dumped all the kit in the boot and climbed into the front. On the way home, he stopped off at a petrol station.

"You want anything?" he asked.

"No, I'm alright, thanks." I did kind of fancy a Crème Egg, but I figured he was just being polite.

He went to the boot, got a metal jerrycan out and started filling it with petrol. When he was done, he put it back and wandered in to pay, emerging a few minutes later with a coffee and a KitKat. He dropped me off at the warehouse, and I collected my 'piece of shit' car and headed home, stopping to buy several Crème Eggs en route.

The next few days passed by uneventfully. I even had a day off; someone else covered my lay-by. I thought a haircut and a panini might be in order – I craved food that wasn't fruit-based. Since I started this job, I'd been unsurprisingly eating a lot more fruit than normal. I was as regular as the head All-Bran taster at the Kellogg's factory.

I drove into town, grabbed a nice stodgy panini and a coffee, and headed down the cobbled streets to the hairdressers'. I sat down to wait my turn in a queue of people, all giving me the 'you know you're after me' look that is traditional in men's barbers. It had been a revelation when in France, a few years earlier, I'd gone to get a trim and discovered that you could make an appointment – apparently women had known this secret for years. Who'd have thought it? I tried it when I got back to England and regretted the phone call almost immediately. The geezer on the end of the phone found it so hilarious he'd shared the joke with the whole barbers.

I grabbed a copy of the local rag from the side for ten seconds of entertainment. I opened the paper and was stunned to see a photo of Arthur, standing next to his precious caravan. The headline read, 'Vandals hit again as caravanning dreams go up in smoke.' Arthur had been at home in bed when he was woken by the flickering lights of Martha (his caravan, not his wife) burning brightly in his driveway. He was devastated, of course, and couldn't see why kids would do something so mindless.

Pool old Arthur, I thought; he loved that tacky monstrosity. It was hard to tell whether his wife would be happy or sad. I wondered if Terry had anything to do with this. It happened on the same night that he dropped me off at home, after stopping for a can of petrol. I got called over for a haircut, and all thoughts of Arthur and his horrific wife were swept out of my head. Soon I was knee-deep in idle chat about holidays and heroic tales of the hairdresser's cocaine-snorting abilities. I wished he'd just cut my hair and shut the fuck up. But from previous experience in these situations, I knew that if I didn't engage with him, he'd start chatting to the other hairdressers and pay even less attention to my hair – the one area in which his meagre skills necessitated his maximum attention.

After agreeing that the back of my head looked excellent, I paid and left.

# CHAPTER 3

# BLOODY CRUSTIES

The next day I'd just finished setting up my stall when my phone rang. It was Hans the German. We hadn't spoken much; he seemed the strong, silent, Germanic type, like a slightly smaller Arnie in *The Terminator*.

"Hi Hans, what's up?"

"James is having trouble at the lay-by, Terry is busy, and I'm stuck in bank. Dave told me to ask you," he said in punctuated English.

"What sort of trouble?"

"Someone try and sell fruit in the lay-by."

"OK, I'll go and have a look. Text me the road it's on."

I hung up and wrote a 'back in five minutes' sign on my stall. I was relieved to get away from the morning of fruit selling and secretly quite happy that Dave had decided I was a better option than all the other sellers to help sort this out.

Ten minutes later and I was at the lay-by in question. A confused-looking James was standing by his car. I'd met him a couple of times in the morning when I picked up my stock for the day. At the other end of the lay-by was a massive white van with a small woman selling fruit and veg from a table. She had a small queue of people and a couple of cars in between us.

"What's happened?" I asked James.

"They were here when I got here," he said, "and they say they aren't moving."

"They?" I asked.

"Yes, there's a fucking massive Rasta down there somewhere, three feral little fucks and a dog that tried to bite me."

"OK, stay here," I said, barely suppressing a laugh.

I walked down the lay-by to their stall. The person in front of me was just buying some potatoes and parsnips. Fruit and veg, now that's a new one. I assumed people only wanted fruit. They paid and walked back to their car.

"Hiya, what can I get you?" said a very posh-sounding tiny lady sporting very dirty thick dreadlocks, with shiny metallic beads on the end. When she moved, they flicked around her head like a grimy Medusa. There seemed to be fewer crusties about these days; they'd become a hard demographic for the unenlightened to spot. The bastard offspring of 70s hippies and New Age travellers, squatters and tree-hugging eco-activists – militant no shit-taking bastard children spawned from the riots of Thatcherism and the free festival scene. But they weren't quite extinct yet; here was a perfect example in the flesh.

A small child appeared at her side, holding her leg through a long grubby-looking floral skirt.

"Nothing, thanks. I'm afraid this is our pitch; we're going to need you to move." I tried to sound as if I had some kind of authority.

"We're not moving. You don't own the lay-by. We know our rights."

Shit, I wasn't prepared for this – what were her rights? What were *our* rights? I just had no idea.

"It's not something I'm going to argue about; we've been selling fruit here for years."

"Well, now we're here, the Magna Carta clearly states that it is legal for any Englishman to sell natural produce at the side of a carriageway."

"Really?" I asked. This suddenly had the stench of bullshit. Whenever someone pulled the Magna Carta card, it was always bullshit.

"Really," she said, looking me straight in the eyes.

"Everything OK, love?" came a deep, bellowing voice from behind the van. A very tall skinny man with massive dreads in a dirty red shirt and jeans emerged from the woods. He was carrying a large armful of muddy potatoes.

"Yes, all perfect, thanks, darling. I was just telling this nice chap what I told the other one – that we're not moving."

The man dumped the potatoes on the stall and stood next to me, staring down menacingly from his lofty position.

"We ain't moving," he said firmly.

"How long were you planning on staying here?" I asked.

"Might be a day, might be a week, maybe all year," he replied.

"Yeah, maybe all year," she echoed.

Two youngish boys ran out to join their father from

the field; they both had Lidl bags full of potatoes.

"I'll give you 'til tomorrow, and if you're still here, we're going to have a problem."

A small dog ran over and started to urinate on my leg.

"For fuck's sake!"

They both laughed and said, "Good boy."

"Tomorrow," I shouted over the traffic, shaking some piss off my leg as I walked back down the lay-by.

I gave Hans a call to update him on the situation, leaving the dog-piss part out.

"Tell James to go home. Me and you deal with them tomorrow. You can fight?" He quizzed.

"Well, I'm no Mike Tyson, but I'll give it a go." Maybe I'd get a big bonus, and besides, I didn't want to come across as a coward with this lot. I suspected that, like a shark, if they smelt my fear, I might get eaten.

I told James to go home for the day; he'd still get paid. He seemed very happy with that. An afternoon of antique programmes and caravan catalogues beckoned its skeletal finger towards him, like a glowing orange David Dickinson of death.

I drove back to my stall; remarkably, nobody had stolen anything, and there was £30 tucked under some strawberries and £30 worth of cherries missing. Was I surplus to requirements?

At university, one of my housemates told me about a job trial he had done when he was desperate for work one skint summer. He'd somehow been convinced to do an unpaid trial day at a meat-packing factory in London, a notion that sounded grim enough by itself. He was given a shovel and taken to a conveyor belt that was emerging through a hole in a wall. His unpaid job for the day, to prove his worth, was to shovel undisclosed meat from the conveyor belt onto another conveyor belt which then vanished through another hole. After a few hours of back-breaking meat-lifting, he was convinced that there were dozens of other people, unpaid and on trial, shovelling meat pointlessly from one conveyer belt to another – a warehouse entirely set up for the bizarre enjoyment of an eccentric millionaire who revelled in the knowledge that the whole operation was completely pointless. As were his victims' meat-shovelling lives. I don't think I was quite there yet, but it flashed into my mind for a second.

The day dragged on in the baking sunshine, being England, it decided to start pissing it down for ten minutes. I sheltered in the car. Minutes later, the sun was back out, and I had two coaches and three carloads of Americans to deal with. Cherries were proving popular today for some reason.

After a busy day, I was pennies shy of two grand. I'd given up texting Dave to tell him my total, his sarcasm drained what little fruit-selling enthusiasm I could muster. I headed home, as I was meeting an old friend, Henry, for a drink. After a quick shower to wash the fruit and petrol off, I was out of the door and down the pub.

It was what most of our friends from across the pond would describe as an "authentic British pub" – wooden beams, roaring fire, medium-quality food, and a couple of drunk racists at the bar. Thankfully, with it being the height of summer, the fire wasn't roaring, but sadly the racists were. I avoided conversation and eye contact with them as I ordered a beer. Despite being inside for most of the time in Spain, I had still come back with a deep tan that would no doubt spark off a predictable line of questioning about 'where I was really from'.

"Adam, over here, mate," came a shout from the back of the bar. I made my way over and found Henry sitting in a small room at a table, clutching a pint.

I hadn't seen him for a couple of years. We'd been close years ago before I moved away. He hadn't changed much, although his once peroxide-blond short hair was now just limp and greying. He was wearing an old Stüssy sweatshirt, which had seen better days. He smiled warmly from ear to ear as I walked in.

"Henry, mate. Great to see you," I said to him.

We had a little man hug. It was genuinely good to see him. We sat and chatted about the good old days, the parties, and our old group of friends. Most of them had either got a few kids and 'real' jobs or had just vanished like me. He seemed genuinely upset by this as if he'd just been waiting for us all to come back so normal fun-times could be resumed.

We weren't too far along this trip down memory lane before our old friend Owl came up. He probably had a real name, but I had no idea what it was. Legend had it that his head could rotate 360 degrees, hence the name. I suspect the irony of his lack of wisdom helped it stick. He was a gigantic cluster fuck of insane wrongness.

"Have you heard from Owl?" I asked.

"Fucking Owl," said Henry, nearly spitting out a

mouthful of beer with his laughter.

"I haven't seen him since the incident," I recalled.

"I have," he sniggered.

"Do tell," I said, sitting back and taking a sip of beer.

The incident was the last time most people had seen Owl. Any sightings were normally just rumours; he was a living urban myth. Years ago, he had been out partying hard as Owl always was. He had also, as always, out-survived everyone he was partying with, which included me and Henry. Everyone was passed out in Henry's living room when the call came in – calls would be more accurate. Everyone in the room's phones started ringing nonstop until we finally awoke from our comatose states. Owl was reportedly going crazy about two miles away inside a kebab shop. The problems (and there were many) were that, firstly, it was 6am and this kebab shop had been shut for hours, and secondly, he had taken a fancy to a large "elephant's leg" kebab.

The wise Owl had solved the first of these dilemmas through the use of a small digger from a nearby building site. He had commandeered the vehicle, driven it a few hundred yards down a busy road and gone straight through the front door of the kebab shop. On the cocktail of drugs he'd ingested over the last forty-eight hours, he had fallen deeply in love with a kebab. He wanted to be with the kebab, despite her (he assured us that he was 100% into women and therefore this kebab was of a female persuasion) imprisonment within the confines of "Best Kebab". One splintered door later, he was naked and had taken the kebab down to a more accessible level.

At this point in the story, the first pair of policemen arrived, just as Owl was attempting to express his love towards the once-rotating mound of meat. It took a further four officers to pry him off, plus another couple and two zaps from a stun gun to get his naked arse in the van. There was now a substantial crowd watching. By the time we got there, it was way too late to help him, and we just saw the van disappearing with him in it.

I'd never seen him again, but his name was everywhere for weeks. The whole city was laughing at him. But Henry had somehow made contact.

"I bumped into him in a little village about forty minutes away, when I was down there working," Henry claimed. "He'd grown a big French moustache and shaved his long hair off. He was wearing an eye patch and farmers' overalls."

"A disguise?"

"Yes, totally," he said, quite excited at the memory. "I could tell it was Owl straight away, though. I saw through his crazy disguise. He was in a café eating at a table where I'd gone to get a coffee."

"What did you do?"

"I sat down next to him and asked him how he was doing"

"And he replied?"

"He fucking did as it happens, mate. I asked him where the fuck he had been, and he said he'd been working on a cider farm down the road. He said he was sorry and begged me not to tell anyone where he was. With that, he stood up and said, 'Merci, au revoir' loudly to the waitress and headed out of the door."

"And that's it?"

"Yes, that's it. I've been back there since, no sign of the fucker."

We both concluded that Owl had evidently never quite recovered. We were probably better off without him; he was a harbinger of chaos.

"Do you want a little livener, mate?" Henry asked, waving a small bag of white powder at me.

"God no," I replied too quickly. He looked offended. "It's just after the last year in Spain, I can't handle even the thought of it anymore."

"Shit, sorry mate, I didn't even think. How was your holiday?"

I loved how everyone called it a holiday, maybe to make me feel better. Spanish jail was anything but.

"Fucking horrible, Henry, I'm trying my hardest not to think about it, to be honest."

"Fair enough, mate. I don't blame you.

"But go on, knock yourself out. Don't mind me," I nodded my approval towards the white bag of cocaine.

"Nice one, mate. Back in a second."

He made off in the direction of Ye Olde Toilet. I finished my beer, bought us both a fresh one, and waited for him to return. He came back refreshed and ready to chat for England. I let him go crazy. He whirred through various hilarious stories about back in the day. After a couple of hours, I was exhausted and made my excuses before heading home. coke made people exhausting if you weren't on cocaine too. It was hard to keep up, and even harder to want to keep up.

I woke up early the next day and made coffee. I headed out to my car and off to the warehouse. I had a baseball bat on the back seat in case of any trouble from the crusties or an unexpected game of rounders. I hoped that they had all fucked off. I massively couldn't be bothered to deal with them. I pulled into the forecourt; Dave and Hans were there already. Hans had a stab-proof vest on and was putting a jacket over the top of it, and Dave was helping him out. I jumped out of the car and said hello.

"Thanks for helping Hans out with this. It won't be forgotten," Dave told me as he passed me a vest. "Just in case."

*In case of fucking what?*

I put the vest on and pulled the Velcro cords tight. I put my hoody on over the top of it. Dave passed me a hammer.

"Er, thanks, I think. I brought a bat," I said, passing it back to him and grabbing my baseball bat from the car.

"Regular fucking boy scout aren't you, Fuck off then," he said with an over-the-shoulder wave as he disappeared inside.

Hans jumped into the passenger seat of my car, and I went round to the driver's side.

"I take it I'm driving, then."

"Yes," he said Germanically.

I started up the car, and off we went.

"What's the plan then?" I asked.

"We go there and make them leave."

45

"Oh, OK, keep it simple then."

"Simple is best."

"Is Dave always so…" I asked, stopping myself mid-sentence.

"So?" asked Hans.

Well, I guess I was committed now. "So cunty. He seems a little cunty."

"That is just how Dave is. I think perhaps he likes you." It was hard to tell if this was German sarcasm.

With that, he turned up the Kraftwerk CD he had just popped in. "Autobahn" blared out of the car's little speakers as we sped down country lanes. A few minutes later, we pulled up in the middle of the lay-by. I was not massively surprised, but more than a little disappointed, to see a large white van with the two crusties setting up their fruit and veg stall.

"Fuck's sake, I really hoped they'd have gone."

"Of course, they not go. Did you really think they would go?" laughed Hans.

He took his Terminator shades off, put them on the dashboard and got out. He was off the moment his feet hit the tarmac. He was already several steps ahead of me, I grabbed my baseball bat from the car and jogged after him with significantly less zeal. The big dreadlocked chap clocked the incoming German ballistic missile.

He dropped the box of vegetables he was carrying and started running towards Hans at full tilt, dreadlocks flowing in the slipstream. They clashed like two fighters in a 90s arcade game. Hans hit him with a claw hammer, but somehow he didn't go down. His momentum knocked a very surprised-looking Hans onto the ground. He sat on top of him, punching him in the face with club-like hands. He'd got two good punches in by the time I arrived.

I paused for a second as I aimed my swing. I was never very good at violence. I tried to avoid it as much as I could. I was always nervous that I'd semi-accidentally kill someone. I could imagine his head exploding like a watermelon. Ridiculous – I doubted I was strong enough even to make an actual watermelon explode, let alone his very solid-looking skull. I changed my swing aim at the last second and smashed him as hard as I could across his chest. He flew backwards off Hans, who was up and on him in seconds.

I heard a screaming noise and felt a whoosh of wind as the small dreadlocked lady leapt through the air onto my chest and started hitting and biting me. She was like a screaming banshee. I staggered around like an on-fire stunt man; I stumbled over to the side of the lay-by and fell into a hedge. My fall was broken by the small batshit-crazy hippy. It seemed to take the wind out of her attack for a few seconds. I grabbed both her wrists and pinned her down. Then with her wind fully back in her sails, she tried to kick me in the balls. I flipped her over and put her arms behind her back. I sat on top of her and looked over at Hans. He was dragging the dreadlocked giant along the floor back to their stall by his hair.

A mulleted child appeared from the hedges and ran at Hans – small though he was, he seemed to have spirit. Hans saw him coming and punted him with a kick that scooped him up like a rugby ball. The child flew through the air, landing deflated in the hedge he had emerged from.

Hans finished dragging the crusty back to his van. A few minutes later, he returned and picked up the hippy by her dreadlocks. He was big enough to keep her at arm's length while she thrashed around and yelled blue murder at him.

He held her with her legs thrashing at him for a few minutes until she stopped spinning and spitting.

"You calm," he asked her.

"Yes," she begrudgingly said after a few seconds.

"Pack up and go now; your man is in the van."

She started to look panicked again.

"He needs first aid, no more spitting or screaming. OK?"

She nodded.

He dropped her on the floor, and she scuttled off back to the van like a beetle.

"Darren, Darren, Darren."

She found Darren. He was slumped over the driver's seat in the van, bleeding and looking defeated.

Hans seemed happy with the situation and headed back to the car.

"OK, we go," he waved me over to the car.

We jumped into the car. He passed me a cigarette as he lit one. He turned on the stereo and cranked up his Kraftwerk CD before putting his shades back on.

The woman had started packing up the stall, and her kids were helping her. She was throwing fruit and veg into the van haphazardly and shouting at them as she did. The kids were copying her and thought it was a game. The big chap was slowly making his way into the van's passenger side, holding a very dirty-looking rag to the side of his head. She finished her super-fast pack-up and slammed the side door shut and ran around and jumped in the van. They sped off, leaving a dust trail and a slightly musty aroma that crusties always seem to leave wherever they go.

Hans called James.

"OK, James, hippies are gone; you come to work now."

And that was that. Hopefully, we'd never hear from them again. I was given the rest of the day off and went home to wash the smell of crusty off. It was as if they'd been using joss sticks left over from the 80s as deodorant. Perhaps they had. The smell surrounded them like a protective force, keeping the bad vibes out and the clean people away.

# CHAPTER 4
# **CREAM**

The next morning, I was back at the fruit. Wimbledon was starting in a couple of days, and this was apparently our busy period. It was all hands on deck. No days off for a couple of weeks, longer shifts and hopefully a lot more money. Strawberry sales were about to go through the roof, according to Dave, who kept gibbering on about 'making hay' and 'all hands to the pumps'. We had to call up when we were running even slightly low; Gregg and a couple of others were out in top-up vans all day and would be with us straight away for a reload.

The sun was already beating down on the hot and pothole-riddled tarmac of my lay-by. There were a couple of big builders' vans at the other end, and there was some activity involving hard hats going down. Two men wearing fluoro Highways Agency vests were walking towards me with a couple of signs. This didn't look good.

"What's going on?" I shouted at them over the traffic.

"Setting up to close one lane today, got to fill a couple of big holes," he shouted back.

Shit, was this bad? I think this was bad. I wanted to smash the takings hard this week – there were bonuses to be had, according to Dave. Not as specific as normal sales bonuses, where you had a target to reach, more of a 'sell some fucking good numbers and I'll sort you out' kind of bonus. I'm not sure a massive traffic jam full of angry tourists was going to help my sales.

I finished setting up and sat and poured myself a coffee. I lit a cigarette and watched the team of builders setting up a couple of traffic lights and an almost endless row of cones. The first few cars pulled past as a man in a yellow jacket waved at them to drive down the single lane. Their windows were wound down, and they all looked over at the fruit stall but couldn't seem to work out if they could stop or not. This was going to be a disaster.

I had an idea. Maybe I should sell directly to the cars? But I needed something smaller and more appealing. I left my stall, leapt into my car, and headed off to the local Co-Op at high speed. I didn't want to leave all that fruit for too long, but hopefully, with a load of builders watching, nobody would steal any. I pulled up on lots of yellow lines, put on my 'honest I'll be back in a minute' hazard lights and ran in. I grabbed a basket, which I filled with single cream, plastic forks, cardboard cups and a few bags of ice. I arrived at the till in record time, just behind an old lady who looked like she might have owned a lot of cats and possibly a piano. She slowly put her basket down and carefully lifted several tins of cat food out (I knew it). She placed each one on the counter very precisely; it looked like it used every ounce of her concentration and strength. Then she put some crumpets down and looked up at the cashier happily.

"Hello, dear."

"Hi, Mrs Wintham, how are you today?"

I was about to explode with pent-up hurry-the-fuck-up-ness, and I think the cashier could sense it.

"That's £7.42, please," she said to Mrs Wintham after scanning everything.

Mrs Wintham suddenly seemed to realise that she might require something to pay with and started to rummage through her handbag for her purse. After pulling out a small grey felt mouse and some extra-strong mints, she finally found it. She opened her purse with a click and pulled out a shiny pound.

Fuck's sake, this could take some time. She counted out her change one coin at a time. The 42p took a while longer.

"I know I've got it in here somewhere," and indeed she did, along with another mint. I put my basket on the end and started to unload my cream and ice.

"Baking a cake, are you dear?" she asked. I'd managed to slow her down even more. Fuck!

"Yes," I said curtly, "and I'm running late with it."

She took her receipt and started to slowly load her cat food into her trolley. At what age do you get one of those trolleys? Where do you buy one from? Do you get a free one when you start drawing your pension?

I paid for my cream and was out of the door before the old lady had even finished packing. I was back at the lay-by in a few minutes. The builders had finished setting up and were having a much-deserved tea break. Nobody had stolen any fruit. Once again, there was some money tucked under a carton, though it was only a tenner this time.

I grabbed my cool box out of the boot and filled it with pots of cream and ice. I opened up the cardboard cups and filled a few with strawberries which I'd hulled with a small knife I had in the car. I poured some cream over the top and stuck a plastic fork in it. Hey, presto 'Wimbledon Specials' - £4 a pop, I reckoned.

I thought I'd make my day easier and took over a tray full of 'Wimbledon Specials' for the workmen to test out. They seemed genuinely touched by the thought and probably needed some food and a sit-down after the gruelling forty minutes of work they'd done so far (including the first tea break).

The traffic was already building up, and there was no time to lose. I loaded up my tray with more specials and walked over to the start of the traffic jam. It was boiling by now, and almost every car had their window open – half of them too tight to turn the air-con on, the other half too stupid to realise it didn't work very well if you tried to cool the whole planet with the windows down.

"Wimbledon Specials, four pounds. Strawberries and cream," I shouted into the first car like a market trader. A confused Deborah Meaden-looking lady on a phone call wound up the window and shook her head at me. But the second car was full of screaming children and was more what I was after.

"Four please," said the dazed-looking dad with one sunburned arm.

I passed them over, and he handed me the cash. The

children stopped screaming and calm descended on the car. I felt like Nanny McPhee.

I moved on to the next car, who bought two, then the next bought three, and then the traffic moved, and I went and filled up.

Within an hour, I'd started to run low on strawberries and cream. I called Gregg for a top-up. "I need a refill, mate, and can you do me a favour and buy me fifty cartons of single cream on the way? I've got the cash here waiting for it."

He seemed confused by my request, but he was a friendly fellow and didn't complain or question it. He turned up thirty minutes later with a tonne of strawberries and loads of cream, which I paid him for. His phone kept constantly ringing with people needing more strawberries. He barely had time for a quick cigarette before he vanished.

"Busy day," he said.

"Fucking Wimbledon," I said like I'd been in the industry for years.

"Yes, fucking tennis. Everyone in England loves tennis and strawberries – why is that?" he asked. "I've been doing this job for years, and I never understand. Fucking weird English."

"They have tennis in other countries, you know," I replied defensively.

"Yes, tennis. But not Wimbledon. Wimbledon is English."

He was right. I had nothing. "Yes, OK, Wimbledon is very English." I'd never properly thought about it before;

I'd foolishly assumed all tennis matches around the world were identical to Wimbledon.

"Still not as English as cricket, surely?" I asked him.

"The bloody cricket," he said in a fake posh English accent. "Even weirder than tennis."

"How about football?" I asked him.

"Yes, football. I fucking love football. I am supporting Arsenal now I live in the UK. Who you supporting?"

"Not really my thing, mate." I instantly regretted being so honest. Telling people you didn't like football, was akin to a teetotaller ordering a lemonade in an Irish bar. It was beyond people's understanding and always made me feel like I was being judged.

"Come on, all you English love football. Beer, shouting, Bobby fucking Charlatan."

"I think it's Charlton," I replied, full of football wisdom.

"Yes, Charlatan. He win World Cup. Everyone love him."

"Yeah, they do, don't they? I'm just not a big sports fan."

He got up and answered his phone. "Yes, OK, OK," he hung up. "Fucking Terry. I've got to go." With that, he flicked his cigarette into the hedge and jogged off to his van.

The day got hotter, and the traffic queue at the lights got bigger. Our new Wimbledon stopping time was 7pm, three hours later than usual. I'd been refilled with cream and strawberries three more times and had taken a truly staggering £4240 by the end of the day. Now that must surely be a record, and more than bonus-worthy.

We all had to bring our takings and left-over stock to the warehouse at the end of each day during Wimbledon. There was a full car park by the time I got there. Dave badly needed to start giving out free sun cream to his staff. They all had the look of a well-cooked plate of gammon and pineapple.

I parked outside on the main street curb, grabbed my money belt and headed over to the open warehouse doors. There was a queue of lay-by workers in front of a table in the middle. Behind the table were Terry and Hans, who were both unsurprisingly drinking yet another espresso. Each worker was handing over bundles of cash, which Terry would pop into a money counter before shouting out the total so that Hans could write it down in a little book. The queue was ten deep, and there were piles of money everywhere. I jumped in at the back. I was starting to realise why they'd snapped me up without much of an interview. There was only one other seller here under the age of sixty. They were all men. They all dressed very similarly, and they all talked about three things almost exclusively:

1.  Caravans. This includes motorhomes. They talked spare parts, new models, engine sizes and upholstery.

2.  Their wives. Her indoors. The ball and chain. These guys were as inappropriate with their views on women's rights as an overweight, chain-smoking, working men's club comedian from the 80s.

3.  Foreign Things. Foreign things were bad. That was the overall vibe. Foreign people, foreign food, foreign

workers. If it wasn't from glorious Britain, then it wasn't for them!

That was it. That was all they talked about. Especially in a small group like this. They weren't quite so bad one-on-one. But let them loose with their own types, and what little social barriers they had were soon let down, like a burst dam of xenophobia and sexism.

Thankfully, Dave soon came stomping down the stairs from his office with Gregg.

"Oi, Cream Boy. Adam!" he shouted at me, "get in here." He beckoned me up the stairs he'd just stomped down, turning around and stomping back up them.

Fuck. Maybe entrepreneurial spirit wasn't what Dave was after. Gregg looked guilty as I passed him on the stairs, as if he'd just grassed me up. But that's OK. I hadn't expected this to be a weird cream-based secret.

"Shut the fucking door."

I did so. "Sorry, Dave, just there was a traffic jam, and I thought I could charge more with cream."

"What the fuck do you think this is? Wimbledon?"

"I took £4240," I said, plonking my money belt down on his desk.

"Well, that's nearly as good as my brother when he used to work for us. Is that after the cost of the fucking cream that you spent my money on?"

"Yes," I said sheepishly.

"Well, it looks like you might be onto something then, doesn't it? I suppose you'll be expecting some kind of fucking bonus."

"No, of course not," I lied, "just doing what I can to

be helpful."

"Fuck off, you twat," he said, passing me £200 from my money belt. He took most of the rest of the cash out and handed the belt back to me.

"See you tomorrow. Shut the fucking door behind you."

Well, that went well enough. As I walked down the stairs, Terry turned towards me as he hung up the call he was on.

"Cream eh – fucking clever cunt. Who'd have thought that would go with strawberries?"

I chuckled, unsure if he was joking or not.

"Dave has my cash," I said to him as I headed out of the warehouse and onto the street.

I got into my car, lit a cigarette, and was about to pull out when a black people carrier cut me off. It swerved across the road and into the warehouse car park. I drove slowly passed the entrance to see who the twat was. The doors of the people carrier all flew open, and four men wearing balaclavas jumped out. One had a sawn-off shotgun, the others metal bars and bats.

What the fuck?

I pulled over and tried to call Dave; my fingers could barely work the phone as the adrenaline took over. I finally managed, and he picked up straight away.

"Dave, you're being robbed, guys with guns in the forecourt."

"Yes, I know, I'm watching them on the cameras. Where are you?"

"I'm outside, I was just leaving."

"Well, I'd be forever in your debt if you could lend a hand." He said calmly.

"Yes, sure. What do I do."

"You got a weapon?"

"I've got the bat from the other day."

"Well, that will have to do, go get it."

I ran to my boot and grabbed the baseball bat. I could hear shouting and chaos coming from the warehouse; a couple of terrified-looking lay-by sellers flew past me with looks of horror on their faces. I peeked around the corner. I could see them in the warehouse. The one with the gun was pointing it at Terry, and the others were herding the staff into a corner. Everyone was shouting. I crept forward into the car park and moved up to the side of the warehouse.

"I see you, son," said Dave. I looked up at one of the cameras. I could hear Terry shouting at someone in the warehouse.

"Go for the big one with the gun when you hear me shout. I'm counting on you, boy; hit him hard, get that gun out of his hands."

I hung up and moved up just outside the entrance, my baseball bat in one sweaty, shaking hand.

I heard a door smash open and Dave's loud, booming voice shout, "Just tell us what you want. No need for anyone to get hurt."

I moved slowly around the corner; everyone's focus was on Dave at the top of the stairs. The big guy was about five metres in front of me. He was waving his gun between Terry and Dave.

I paused. I wanted to run the other way. Fuck fruit selling. Fuck these people. Fuck…

I ran towards the trouble, both hands firmly grasping the bat, which was swung back, ready for the pitch. I crossed the ground in seconds. He saw me at the last of them. But it was too late. I swung the bat hard. No second thoughts about watermelons this time. I hit the gun and the hand he was supporting the sawn-off barrel with. As it flew out of his hands, he instinctively pulled the trigger. The noise exploded in the metal-walled warehouse, as did an enormous pile of fruit next to Terry.

For a second, everyone froze, and time slowed down. Strawberries flew in slow motion through the air. A large red splatter hit Dave on the nose as he pulled a handgun from behind his back. Terry was on top of the now slightly less threatening larger one whose hand I had just pulverised.

Two shots rang out. The whole place went silent.

Dave stood at the top of the stairs, gun in hand. He slowly descended, pointing the gun with both hands at two of the invaders at the bottom of the stairs. Nobody seemed to be hit; he must have fired into the air.

"You come in my fucking warehouse with one fucking gun… One fucking gun."

He seemed genuinely insulted that they hadn't brought more weapons.

On reaching the bottom of the stairs, he turned towards the first man. He dropped his metal bar on the floor nervously as Dave approached. The noise it made echoed around the silent and tense room. Dave shot him once in the knee, and he dropped to the floor, screaming.

"Fucking cunts, who fucking sent you then?" he punctuated the question with a gun barrel in the mouth.

Terry proceeded to punch the big guy unconscious with a giant knuckle-duster-covered fist as if to emphasise that they wanted answers. Was shooting one of them not enough? I quietly moved to the side of the warehouse; hoping that my time contributing to this situation had passed.

"Everyone without a balaclava on, fuck off outside," Dave said.

There were three or four fruit unpackers and about ten terrified-looking old lay-by sellers still watching. They didn't need telling twice; I hadn't seen old people move that fast since M&S accidentally priced up their gammon joints for 1p, and word got out down the bingo.

"So, shall we take our masks off and get better acquainted?" Dave asked the next one, pushing the side of his balaclava up with the end of his handgun.

They didn't move, more out of fear than arrogance.

He shot the same guy in the other knee. His legs were fucked. He started making a weird whimpering noise.

"Drop the fucking sticks and take the fucking masks off," shouted Terry, who'd picked up the sawn-off shotgun and was holding it at the groin of the unconscious man on the floor.

They took their masks off. I recognised one of them immediately. It was the cunt with the scar on his face, the fucking pirate. Terry looked overjoyed and had a hand on his zip in seconds.

"You… You fucking pissing little cunt," he shouted, pushing the gun into his teeth. "On your knees, you Cornish prick."

He fell to his knees just as Terry started pissing. The look on his face was one of pure relief and happiness as he pissed all over his head and shoulders. When he was done, he zipped up and smashed him around the side of the head with the shotgun butt. He hit the floor hard; piss and blood trickled down his unconscious forehead.

"Three down, one to go," said Dave walking over to the last man standing. He cowered on the floor.

"Can you drive?" he asked him.

"Wh…What?" he stammered.

"Can you fucking drive?"

"Yes, yes."

"Get in the car and take these pricks with you then."

He nodded and started dragging the guy with the two shot knees over to the people carrier. He pushed him into the back and then went back to help the piss-covered one up. Terry looked like he wanted to keep him. He had the look of a cat losing his new mouse.

"Come on, Terry," said Dave, patting him reassuringly on the shoulder. "You've pissed on him and broken his jaw."

"OK, OK."

He had two of them in the car now and came over for the big one.

"Wait," said Dave.

He walked over to the big man, who was starting to get up. He kicked his knee and knocked him back to the ground. He stood over him with one foot on his chest, aiming his gun at his head with both hands.

"Tell your fucking boss this is his last chance to stop being a cunt. Stay the fuck out of this area, or we'll be down for him. Got it?"

He nodded and murmured yes.

Dave took his foot off and turned towards the others. Changing his mind mid-turn, he spun back and shot him in the foot.

"Just so you don't forget."

He staggered over to the car's passenger door, and they backed up out of the warehouse, with Terry pointing the shotgun at the passenger window as they went.

They sped off down the road.

I lit a cigarette, dragging on it hard. My mind was going at a million miles an hour. This definitely wasn't what I signed up for.

"Fucking pirates," said Terry happily.

"Good work, lad, good work. You might be up for employee of the week at this rate," Dave said to me, waving towards an 'employee of the week' corkboard with an old picture of Les Dennis on it. There was a dart in his forehead.

I had no words.

They let me go home while they cleared up the mess. The adrenaline was something else. I'd seen a few guns in my life, but never anything like that. I was buzzing with energy for the rest of the night. No chance of sleep. I went for a walk around the local park to clear my head. I felt like a young Darth Vader, I could feel myself getting a taste for the darker, more criminal side of life. I'd spent half my life occupying somewhere between normal life and the criminal world. It was inescapable, always lurking just under the soft rice pudding skin of normality. Perhaps I should just embrace it.

I headed home at about 4am and managed a couple of hours of restless sleep, filled with nightmares of giant cherries chasing me up trees with shotguns.

# CHAPTER 5

# CLIMBING THE LADDER

The next day when I arrived at the lay-by after barely sleeping a wink, Terry was waiting for me. He had a cool box at his feet and a big grin (or something closely resembling one) on his face.

"Beers?" I wondered out loud.

"No, fucking cream, you twat. We've rolled out your Wimbledon Specials today to all the lay-bys – thought I'd drop your cream and cups off and deliver the news."

"Brilliant stuff."

"And well done for last night; you saved our collective arses. It hasn't gone unnoticed. Dave says to make sure you pop by and see him at the end of the day when you drop off your cash."

"No problem."

With that, he was off and away.

I picked up the cool box and moved it over to where I was about to set up. I popped it open, it had several litre bottles full of cream and some loose ice in it. I guess that would do it; there was a big Sports Direct bag full of wooden forks and paper cups too. I opened my boot and started to set everything up. I noticed a metal poster board at the side of the road; Terry must have forgotten to mention it. It read, "Wimbledon Special, Strawberries & Cream – £4."

There was already a queue at the temporary traffic lights. I sold a few to the first couple of cars. The next was a big white minibus crammed full of people. It edged forward towards me, and the driver wound down the window. The Chemical Brothers poured out onto the road. I said hello, and the whole minibus replied enthusiastically; they were all Londoners. They all looked off their heads, massive eyeballs everywhere.

"What you got, mate?" they asked.

"Strawberries and cream."

Several approving noises came from the back. The driver looked the worst of the bunch. He was sweating a lot.

"You OK, mate?" I felt obliged to ask him.

"Not bad mate, not bad, bit cream-crackered though. Long night with this lot at a party."

"Yeahhhh party!" came from the back.

"How much are they, geezer?" asked the woman in the passenger seat.

"Four quid," I told her.

"Yeah, big old party," continued the driver obliviously.

"You alright to drive all the way to London, mate? It's a long way."

"What's that?" laughed one of the passengers, "a fucking long 'un for some strawberries?"

"No, I've got them right here," I told her, slightly losing where this was all going.

"They can't be more than a diver," said the driver. "A fucking long un, for real?"

I was totally lost in a sea of cockney rave banter.

"Mate, you're taking the piss," shouted someone from the back. "A hundred quid for a strawberry because we're miles from London."

I gave in. "Here you go, have one for free," I said and thrust a portion of strawberries and cream through the window and walked off.

With that, they turned up the music and drove off. What the fuck was that all about? I never could understand cockneys. These weren't the posh Chelsea set that I normally got here. More salt-of-the-earth types. They made even less sense, although they were at least normally friendly, unlike the posh ones.

£5800 and one exhausting day later, I headed off to cash out and pop in on Dave. He was outside when I arrived and waved me into a smaller car park around the side. As I parked, he disappeared through a door, waving me to follow him. I entered the warehouse into an office I hadn't seen before. It was a bit more luxurious than the upstairs one, with leather sofas and a large antique desk. He sat down behind it and slammed his hands down on the table.

"Wimbledon Special! Fucking genius, well done. It's gone very well. We took about thirty percent more today than the day before, and that was a pretty busy one. You've done well, Adam. You fucking stepped right up during that robbery too; not sure how that would have ended if you hadn't been outside." Interesting that he thanked me for the Wimbledon Special first and not saving his life, I thought. It was clear where Dave's priorities lay.

He pulled a folder from a drawer in his desk; it looked like one of those files that the FBI have in films. It had my name on it and a photo of me pinned to the front. He opened it up. "So, tell me a bit about yourself," he said, slightly menacingly.

I had no idea where to start or why he was asking. Maybe his folder just had my CV in it. Let's start with that. I ran him through the usual bullshit: A-levels, university, work experience at yadda yadda, worked for a year at blah blah and always dreamed of working in the food industry.

"Well, that's very interesting," he yawned while scrunching my CV into a ball and throwing it into the bin. He pulled out several other pieces of paper and started to flick through them, tutting and occasionally chuckling to himself.

"What do you want, Adam? What interests you?"

"I like walking and music," I suggested.

"Of course you fucking do, son," he laughed. "And what else have you been up to before you started here?"

"I lived in Spain for a bit."

He read over another document. "It says here that you were arrested for intent to supply while you were at university, but all charges were later dropped due to lack of evidence."

What the fuck? I felt my heart rate double; all I could manage to say was, "What, when?"

"There's more, lots more," he chuckled, flicking through the pages.

"How did you... That isn't meant to be on my record," I stammered.

"Depends which records you're looking at, I guess. I see Spain was more of a *special holiday* than you just living there for a bit."

"Well, I did have some problems in Spain."

"Problems," he laughed. "I'm not sure being caught with half a kilo of coke and assaulting two policemen is just a problem."

I turned white. How the fuck did he know about that?

"It was all a misunderstanding," I said truthfully.

"How so?" asked Dave.

"Firstly, the two policemen were undercover. I didn't know they were police."

"Oh, I bet," he said sarcastically.

"I was just sitting in a square waiting for my friend. I was smoking a little spliff which normally nobody cares about over there. Suddenly these two Spanish guys jump on me while walking past. I thought I was being robbed, so I punched one of them in the face and legged it."

"And the cocaine? That's quite a bit of blow to be sitting around with."

"Well, yes, that's where it gets a bit embarrassing. My friend had left his bag with me. I had no idea what was in it. I didn't even know he sold coke. First thing I knew about it was when the undercovers caught up with me and opened the bag of his I had with me."

"But they didn't believe it was his bag, I take it."

"I couldn't say anything. I'm not a grass. I told them it was mine."

"So you just took it on the chin for your amigo, did you?"

"Yes. Stupid, really, I know. A year and a bit later, here I am. I take it you're going to fire me."

"It's alright, don't start stressing," he said, seeing me on the verge of a full meltdown. "You see, the thing is, we're not looking for the average member of staff here. We are looking for people with a slightly different life perspective."

"Is this a job interview? Are you offering me a new job?" I asked hopefully.

"Well, perhaps I am. I think we can both agree you might be a little wasted in a lay-by selling fruit."

"I might be saving up for a caravan."

"You fucking might at that," he replied.

"I kind of just thought I could have a relaxing summer selling some fruit while I sorted my head out," I told him honestly. "You know, try and become a normal member of society, get a job, that kind of thing."

"And this was what you came up with? God help you if this is your idea of a respectable job in the normal world."

"It's a start."

"Indeed. Anyway, here is a little thank-you for your idea and your help the other day with that spot of bother." He pulled out what looked like about a grand, and tossed it over to me.

"Thanks, that's very generous of you. What exactly would this new role involve?"

"Less day-to-day selling and more logistics. Ideas, merchandise tracking, team management, that kind of thing; some of it legit, some of it," he waved my file at me, "less so. We lost someone a few months ago, and Terry has been filling in. But he lacks a certain finesse, and he'd be the first to admit that security is more his thing."

"You need a lot of security selling strawberries?"

"Well, exactly," he said with a worrying lack of sarcasm. "We need someone who can deal with customers, the suppliers and the selling teams. It's a varied role, definitely more interesting than flogging fruit at the side of the road all day, which for a man with your CV must be a little dull."

"Well, sometimes dull can make a nice change," I said.

"The pay would be significantly more. Have a think and let me know after the weekend if you want."

"I will. Thanks very much for the offer and the bonus," I said.

My head was spinning as I left the office. What kind of fruit-based criminal underworld had I got myself involved in? I shut the door behind me and lit a cigarette, breathing deeply. This might be what a panic attack feels like, I thought as I slipped into a mild panic attack. How did a man with a penchant for summer fruits know so much about me? I didn't even have an official record. What else was in that file? Where the fuck did he get that information from? After Spain, I wanted to just have an easy summer. Spanish jail was hardly a holiday. It was a hot, sweaty shithole. I just wanted some time without any stress, cockroaches or greasy Spanish food.

I climbed into my car and sat back, enjoying all the benefits of the rest of my Benson. For all Dave's faults and weirdness, at least he wanted to give me a raise and a new job. Normally when your boss finds out about your murky past, they fire you, so he can't be all bad.

I started the car. "Stand and Deliver" by Adam and the Ants came galloping out of the stereo. I turned it up, wound down the window and drove home confused and surrounded by stories of Dandy Highwaymen.

I had a lot to think about over the weekend but no time to think about it. Wimbledon was upon us, and I had created some kind of cream-based monster, which was taking over lay-bys across the South of England. I wonder how much cream we were getting through a day now – a good few cows' worth, surely.

Saturday was a baking hot blur of caravans and coaches full of tourists. I had a rare coachload of Americans who entertained me for a while. Back in the 80s, you couldn't move for them. These days, they mostly travelled in cars and not in packs. These were some proper old-fashioned Reagan-style republicans from Florida. They were all called Robert, Barbara or Kathleen, and were the opposite of old English Tories, who I guess are their equivalent.

The posher you got in England, the more polite and reserved you seemed to get as you got older, until, with luck and a good diet, you turned full Mary Berry. But in America, you apparently got louder and dumber, as did your clothes.

They regaled me with tales of alligators on golf courses and how delicious their crabs were, and I soon remembered why the rest of the world hated Americans so much in the late 80s. It wasn't just their occasional invasion of other countries, but the loud, obnoxious, dumb tourists that did it.

The temporary traffic lights were still up, although thankfully the workmen were no longer around. They'd vanished quickly without touching the holes they came to fix. I was selling so much fruit that Dave had sent me a new helper to maximise the profit potential (his words, not mine). He had just finished his first year at uni and was called Keiron. He was enthusiastically clueless, and so had the potential to fit right in. I put him on strawberry cup-making duties and saved myself the constant walking back and forth. The weekend traffic was insane – the tailback from the roadworks was a couple of miles in each direction.

People honked, stereos blared, and strawberries were sold. The great thing about the traffic jam was that by the time cars got close enough for me to sell them strawberries, they were nearly out of it, meaning they were much happier than they had been an hour before at the other end of the jam. At the far end, they were pissed. The fruit and cream seemed like a celebration of their having made it through to the other side. Nearly every car bought some; it was never-ending, we were selling about four pots a minute. I did the maths. Two hundred and forty an hour multiplied by ten hours, at £4 a pop, equalled £9600

It was hard work, by lunchtime, I was hot, sweaty and covered in strawberry juice. Keiron was looking like he was waning slightly. Kids today have no work ethic, I thought for a second. Then realised I sounded like one of the caravanners and backtracked myself mentally.

We took a short break; I poured us both a coffee and gave him a fag. I wondered if he'd be taking over my pitch if I took Dave up on his offer. Was he capable of keeping up the pace, or would he crumble? It could go either way, I thought as he spilt coffee down his t-shirt.

He was studying business and was saving up to go travelling in India. I filled him with stories of generous cash bonuses and the fun to be had inhaling endless car fumes while selling stolen fruit. I didn't quite put it like that, of course. I didn't want to scare him off. I bored him with my theories on the business world too.

"Nobody succeeds in business unless they are ripping someone off or doing something illegal or terrible," I explained to him, while he looked concerned.

"Which are we doing here?" he asked, quite reasonably.

"We're just selling fruit, mate," I laughed. He laughed nervously with me. Well, this was going well. "OK, back to work." Chats like this made me realise that perhaps I wasn't for mass consumption. Imagine if I worked in an office — I'd be shunned in about ten minutes. The moment I opened my mouth, the game would be up.

I remember an old friend of mine called Bobby. He wasn't for mass consumption, either. He blagged a fancy new job in Canada years ago. He packed up his life and flew over there; some of his new work team even met him at the airport. He wanted to go to the hotel and sleep, but they suggested a pint to get to know each other. Wonderful, he thought. I love pints!

Several pints later, he found himself back at his hotel with little memory of what had just happened. It must be the jet lag, of course! The next morning, he made his way to his new job. He was buzzing despite being exhausted and hungover. Sadly, he hadn't made quite the James Bond impression on his future work colleagues that he imagined he had. In fact, the impression he had made was so earth-shatteringly terrible, that he never made it further into the building than the reception desk. Two large security guards were waiting for him, and he was ejected from the building and told never to return. He flew home with a hangover, no job and no house. I hoped I was slightly less socially inappropriate, but there was no guarantee.

By 6.30 that evening, we were both on our last legs, and Dave's job offer seemed more appealing by the second. I didn't know and could only imagine what the job might really entail. But anything was better than putting myself through another Saturday trying to sell this many strawberries. I was sick of the taste and the smell of them. Cherries seemed like a thing of the past. I hadn't sold any for days. I missed cherries, the cream-free simplicity of them, the distinct lack of stickiness and their refreshing lack of smell. The fruit was getting to me.

We decided to call it a day. I gave Keiron a lift back into town as he was car-less (I wonder how he got to the lay-by in the morning). I congratulated him on a job well done and told him we had taken nearly £7000. I said I'd have his wages and a little bonus the next day and he ambled off quite happily, thoughts of his exotic travels in his head. He seemed like the kind of naïve young chap that comes back from India with a distant stare, a fear of dogs, and an interesting scar shaped like Jesus.

I had more important things to worry about, though. I'd come to a realisation today, for all my supposed desires to be more normal, settle down a bit, get my head together, and enter the rat race. It all seemed like a lot of hard work for fuck-all reward. Maybe I was as spoilt as the young lads that I always heard the other sellers moan about.

I called Dave.

"Adam, how are you doing?" he answered, sounding surprisingly cheerful.

"Yeah, good, just under seven k today. Keiron was a lifesaver."

"Good, good. Head back to the warehouse to cash out. I'm not in, but Terry is."

"I'd like to take you up on your offer. If it still stands?"

"Good lad, I knew you would. Have tomorrow off and come in Monday at eight sharp. You won't regret it."

People only said that if they knew you'd probably regret it.

I hung up and was just glad I didn't have to put myself through another day of strawberry-selling tomorrow. I was slightly worried as to how Keiron would get on without me. Hopefully, they'd give him someone good to help.

I drove to the warehouse. My air-con was shot, so I wound all the windows down. It was a sticky, muggy evening. The streets were deserted and every pub I drove past was packed. Was the football on, I never seemed to get the memo. I pulled into the industrial estate just as some heavy rain began, the air instantly cleared and it started to pour down. I drove into the warehouse car park and pulled up near the front doors to avoid the crazy rain.

Terry was standing in the middle of the open doors, sipping an espresso. He grinned as I ran over to the doors and was instantly soaked. I was so hot, I quite enjoyed it, but I didn't let him know, as he seemed happy by my potential wet misery.

"Coffee?" he asked.

"Yeah, sure, why not?"

He walked over to the staff coffee machine and made me an espresso.

"Busy day?" I asked him. "How's the cream gone?"

"Yeah, very good," he said, giving me a sideways glance.

"You already got your bonus?"

"Yeah, I got it, don't worry, I'm not after another one, just interested."

"Fair enough," he chuckled. "Yes, we smashed it. The biggest day of the year so far. Bigger than any last year too."

I chucked him my money belt, and he took the cash out and counted it. I threw him a couple of stacks I had in my backpack too.

He put the cash in bundles and made a note of the totals.

"So you took the job then?"

"Yeah."

"Well, I hope you're up to it."

"We'll see. How hard can it be?"

He looked up at me as if I was crazy. I was going to have to stop saying this to people.

I put my finished coffee on the table and said my goodbyes. "I need some sleep. See you Monday."

"No problem, see you Monday. Welcome aboard."

The storm had passed. I got in my freshly cleaned car and sped off for home.

When I got back, I smoked a spliff and wondered what I had just gotten into. I was fairly sure they weren't up to anything more than selling slightly dodgy fruit, though I couldn't help but wonder if it was a cover for some kind of drugs operation. But after an attempted robbery and a fight with some crusties, it seemed like fruit was more than enough to keep this lot busy.

Maybe if I kept my head down and helped them make even more money, it would all be OK. Perhaps this was the kind of job that I'd been looking for my whole life. Dodgy enough to keep me interested, but straight enough to be a "real job".

I passed out on the sofa stinking of strawberries and off cream – Eau De Lay-By by Chanel.

# CHAPTER 6

# A TRIP TO THE COUNTRY

A day off. No fruit. No petrol fumes. No tourists. I had a relaxing day watching films and smoking weed planned. It was scorching hot, probably the hottest day on record since time began; the day everyone had been waiting for through ten years of dreadful summers that felt like a Russian winter.

I made a coffee and thought about how lucky I was to be off for the day. I went to roll a spliff and realised my stocks were down to crumbs. I hadn't been paying attention to THC supply levels. I made a sad spliff with a few speckles of weed, knowing I was going to have to go and see Mike. He was my only reliable contact since I came back to the area. He was also the only person who'd be in on a day like this. He hadn't left the house for about a year by his reckoning. But then he did have a fucking enormous house.

I reluctantly grabbed my keys and headed out and into the car. You didn't need to call ahead with Mike. He didn't have a mobile and never answered his landline. He had an answering machine from the nineties with a little cassette that recorded messages, which he screened through an enormous sound system. The tape was full of awkward, posh stoners leaving paranoid messages for him. He'd play it back to me when we were stoned and laugh at how stupid they all sounded.

He was a strange type, a true authentic, the kind of person you'd find on the drug fringes of America, living in a house in the desert made of tyres with a pack of dogs and a terrifying wife. There was also something about him that made him inherently English – a unique combination indeed.

After about twenty minutes, I pulled onto the long country road that led to his house. It was a claustrophobically high-hedged winding country nightmare with occasional tiny passing points of a road. Thankfully I managed to make it the whole way without encountering a lorry. Result! Last time I had to reverse about half a mile.

I pulled into his driveway and pressed the intercom at the big black metal gates. A camera spun around and looked at me.

"Yessssssss," came a strange Dracula-like impersonation down the crackly intercom.

"It's me, you bellend. Open up."

"The master will see you," he said, laughing maniacally at the end for good measure.

It was only half-eleven in the morning. Even strange people weren't normally strange this early.

The gates creaked open. I had my suspicions that he'd added the creaking noise as a sound effect – I don't remember them creaking like that before. I drove up his drive, which curved through a shambolic garden of overgrown bushes and once gloriously trimmed and shaped trees. I parked outside his sprawling stone farmhouse. The wooden window frames needed some love, and the odd tile was sliding off the roof. The ivy that covered most of the house had probably gone past the charming-looking stage and into the 'destroying your home' phase. As if the main house wasn't large enough, it had a huge old stable yard attached to it. It was a proper rural retreat, all made out of the local stone; the look was, I believe, "rustic equestrian". He'd bought it at auction years ago. It was made for him, with plenty of room to grow weed, no neighbours to freak out and enormous gates.

A rare find by a rare specimen.

The door flew open, and a tall, semi-naked, pot-bellied bearded man in a pair of worryingly tight white pants and a silk lady's dressing gown emerged from within.

"Adam, hombre, good to see you, man," he said, pulling me into a tight hug. Long ago, he lost all normal social boundaries through a life of extraordinarily strong weed and voluntary social isolation. I noticed he had a massive black eye as soon as he released me from the overly long, all-too-naked hug.

"Where did you get the shiner, mate?"

"I'll tell you in a bit." He took a drag on a frankly terrifying-looking spliff. It was about eight inches long and full of ill intent.

"Did you start your new job yet?" he asked.

"Yes, been doing it a little while now."

"What's the work world like after your little holiday in Spain?"

"Anything is better than that, mate."

"I bet. Only a dopey cunt like you would go on holiday and end up stuck out there for all that time."

He had a cheek calling me a dopey cunt. But he did have a point.

"Yes, you're probably right. Maybe this job will get my life back on track."

"Ah yes," he said, taking a drag on the enormous cone.

"Camberwell carrotting again, are you?" I asked him.

"Yeah, man. When in Rome..." he said, passing it over to me.

That probably meant something in his head, I thought as I took a large drag.

"How are the kids?" I asked.

"Come check them out, man. They are so fucking beautiful."

He dragged me over towards the old stable block. He had a couple of horses and would ride them high around his fields. The place was a sprawling estate filled with crumbling outbuildings and endless fields.

We went into one of the outbuildings. There was a row of four stables in a corridor with wooden half-height doors going into each one. The place stunk of horse shit. It was a bit too warm for this. Two horses poked their heads out of the second and third stables. The nearest was a beautiful brown-haired number. Mike stroked her head and put his other hand out on the black chap who was looking jealously on from next door. I wasn't really horsey, but his horses were always very nice. I occasionally wondered if he fed them weed, and they were, in fact, high horses. But it's not something you could ask someone like Mike straight out.

He opened the door to the black horse's stable, and we walked in. He made his way to the back wall and pressed a button on a key ring, and a little door slid open in the stone wall. He ducked down and made his way in, and I followed. We emerged into a small room. He moved a rug out of the way and yanked up a metal door in the floor. He flicked on a light switch and descended down a ladder into the depths.

I followed him down about ten metal rungs. As we got lower, I could hear The Orb's "Little Fluffy Clouds" playing. We landed on a metal grid floor with a clang.

"Behold their beauty," he said.

We looked out over a large underground space. It was low-ceilinged but enormous. Tables were laid out all around the outside and down the centre in rows. On them were about two-hundred cannabis plants, all of them about three feet tall and laden with big, heavy buds. The whole place was glowing blue from all the lights, and large fans whirred away, gently blowing the heavy, sticky smell around the room. The ceiling was a maze of extraction pipes, sucking the smell off to god knows where. It was quite the setup.

"They're nearly ready," he said proudly.

"Why the Orb?" I asked.

"Just this track. They love this track."

"Not fans of their later work?"

"No, I tried a whole album. They only peaked chemically when this track was played."

Mike had told me about this before. He'd measure chemical levels in their leaves as he played different music to them. He was convinced they reacted to the music, which affected their growth. He was as mad as a very stoned March hare. But he did grow the finest weed I had ever tasted, so I guess he got a pass.

"What else are they into?"

"Well, the usual – James Brown and anything funky," he stated matter-of-factly.

He sprayed a plant near him with a little water sprayer and examined the buds. "Look, they're the best yet," he said, beckoning me down to his level. He passed me a small magnifying lens. I took it and peered through it at the bud.

"Look at those crystals – biggg crystals."

I could actually see crystals. Normally I couldn't see shit and just nodded politely. I stood up and went to light the spliff.

He snatched it out of my mouth. "Not in front of them, man. It's not right. It's like taunting a cow with a burger."

"Fair enough," I laughed. "Let's go to your house then and leave these beautiful creatures to it."

"They are beautiful, aren't they? Beaut-i-ful."

I climbed back up the ladder, out through the room, and into the stable. I patted the horse as I passed. He really did look high.

We headed into his house. I noticed that the front door

had a smashed lock.

"So, about time you told me about that eye, mate? Is the door anything to do with it?"

"I guess so," he said, whipping us up a couple of coffees. "Some little fuckers robbed me last week."

"No way, fuck off. How did they get in?"

"One of my twice-a-year customers... they came in the backseat of his car. I couldn't see them on the camera. He owed them a load of money for some white, and this was his clever way of paying them back. I buzzed him in and he came up the drive. The moment he got up here, I could see something wasn't right and dashed back inside. I bolted the door, thought I was maybe OK for a second, and then they smashed it down with one of those police battering rams."

"Who the fuck has one of those knocking about?"

"Ian Mathews, that's who."

"That rings a bell. Is he one of those brothers?"

"Yeah, that's the one. They sent me flying with their police thing and then ran in and hit me in the eye with the end of a gun."

"What kind of gun?"

"I don't know. I'm not a gun person. Big shiny-looking pistol type of thing."

"A handgun? Ouch."

"Yes, fucking ouch. Better than being shot, though, I guess."

"Well, that's very Zen of you," I said, lighting up a new spliff I'd just rolled from his tray on the kitchen table. "They clearly didn't get your babies, did they?"

"They were looking for them, but I don't show every Tom, Dick and Harry my babies – you're one of the lucky ones."

"I'm honoured."

"They wanted my weed. They knew where I kept my in-house stash and went straight to the compartment. They grabbed about three or four kilos from there. They made me open the safe. I had about fifteen k in there."

"Fuck man, that's a fucker."

"Then they started asking me about the plants. I told them I'd just harvested, and that was it. I even showed them the old grow room which I still haven't cleared out yet."

"I knew that lazy streak would come in useful in the end. And that was that?"

"Pretty much. I had to pay some old friends to go and visit my now very ex-customer."

"I take it you couldn't find Ian?"

"No, he's easy to find, but it turns out he's untouchably connected. Him and his brothers, I could take you to where they live now. But I can't do shit!"

"Connected, with who, the La fucking Cosa Nostra?"

"Well, no, but they run all the scag and white for miles. The Mathews Clan, they call themselves – there's fucking loads of them. Brothers and uncles, a whole family of cunts. There was some terrifying mother who ran the whole thing. She was a proper nasty piece of work. She died last year. Since then, they all went feral. She was the only one who could keep them all under control."

He passed me another enormous spliff he had just

made.

"Good lord," I said, taking a deep drag. "You don't know anybody that will fuck with them?"

"No, not a soul. Honestly, I got a black eye and lost a few quid. They missed about four hundred k of nearly finished weed, so I guess I got off lightly."

"That, my friend, is, as always, a very philosophical way of looking at it."

"Zen master level nine, mate, don't fuck with me," he said, taking a drag of another monster spliff.

"You going to beef up your security?"

"Yeah, just got a load of perimeter cameras and some sensors and also these." He pulled out two small black Uzis from under the counter. I couldn't believe my eyes.

"What the fuck, mate? Is that an Uzi?"

"Yeah, man – I fucking got Uzis, motherfucker," he said in an American accent while pointing them at me sideways.

"That's totally mental mate."

"Anyway, what are you after?" He pulled a large pair of industrial scales out of a drawer.

"Usual, please, mate."

He took a few bags of different skunk out of various cupboards and weighed me up a couple of bags.

"That'll be two hundred, my man."

I passed over the money. "Thanks, mate. You are, as always, a fucking lifesaver."

"I forgot, man. I haven't even shown you the best bit. One of my clients is a bit of an engineer. You know the type, glasses and secret weed habit. Anyway, he knocked me this up and had it constructed off-site to pay off a medium-sized debt he had with me."

We walked to the front door. On closer inspection, it was pretty fucked. You could see where the battering ram had hit it and how it had been put back up after being ripped off its hinges.

"Well, I hope you don't mean the door, as I think you might want a refund."

"Not the door. I got a new one of them coming tomorrow. Stand back over there as if you were about to try and come in."

I stood a few feet down the path, and Mike closed the door on me. I heard him thump a button. A massive metal door came down with a whoosh just in front of his fucked front door. It smashed down to the ground at a worrying speed with a thunderous noise. A metal shutter crashed down in front of the window next to the front door. To top it off, a small hatch opened in the door, and an Uzi tip popped out.

"Say hello to my little friend," Mike said, sticking his head out of the hole and laughing.

"Impressive mate, fair play – you've excelled yourself."

"Yeah, it's the shit, man," he shouted through the hole.

The door and window shutters whooshed back up into their holes smoothly.

"Cool, eh?" he said. "Anyway, I've got to go feed the horses, amigo, so time for you to offski."

"No worries, I'm probably way too stoned to be driving, but fuck it."

"You can borrow a horse if you want."

"That would most definitely not help in any way."

"See you soon, man, take care," Mike said, and with that, he was off towards the stables.

I slowly got into my car, hid the bag of goodies under the front seat and made my way out of the compound and back home. For once, I was glad that it was a very scenic route to his house. Minimal chance of meeting any police.

I got home and made a spliff from the bag of delights. I had an early night and slept like a very stoned horse.

# CHAPTER 7

# REGIONAL LAY-BY MANAGER

My alarm woke me up at seven. I fell off the sofa where I'd passed out. I showered, got ready, and headed in with mildly concerning thoughts about what my future with the slightly unnerving Dave, Terry and Hans might hold. I pulled in at about five to eight, round the side to the new and somewhat more VIP car park. It was hardly complimentary champagne and people ushering you through rope barriers, more a slightly less strong odour of rotting fruit and fewer bin liners full of plastic supermarket boxes.

I knocked and walked in.

Dave was sitting at his big antique desk with Terry to one side. Hans was perched slightly awkwardly on the side of a small coffee table, sipping an espresso in a suit that seemed like it may not have been his, or he'd grown a lot recently. He was rocking an orange roll-neck jumper today, which was quite the look with the tight grey suit. He was fantastically German, and I couldn't work out if I should be scared of him or discussing 80s hits by David Hasselhoff. It felt like maybe Hans didn't know either.

"Morning. Grab a seat," Dave said, waving me towards

a chair.

"So, what am I going to be doing?" I asked.

Dave explained that they were expanding the operations this year and needed someone to help in a few areas. There were two main aspects to the business that I'd be involved in initially: lay-by management and product sourcing. The rest of the company was mostly cash management and security, which was what Terry and Hans were here for. Terry crossed over into lay-by management a little. Gregg, the Polish lad, also dealt with some of the product sourcing and logistics involved in that side of the business.

It was starting to sound a bit businessy all of a sudden. I imagined it would be more crime-based after that interview. I don't know if I was relieved or disappointed. I was starting to realise that I quite liked the buzz from the crime element. I was half-expecting Dave to flick over a white paper chart and start pointing at graphs and brainstorming with Hans, but luckily they didn't go down that route.

"By sourcing, do you mean stealing?" I asked.

"Well, no, we pay for everything, don't worry – we're not sending you out on the rob."

"We're fully legit," added Terry, making the whole thing sound even less so.

Dave told me that today I was to go and introduce myself to all the lay-by teams, and then this evening, me and Gregg would be heading out for some product sourcing. Terry passed me a clipboard with all the names and addresses of everyone on the lay-by teams. There were several pages of them; a few had sad faces drawn next to them and others had hand-scribbled notes.

"What's with the sad faces, Terry?" I asked.

"People we are fucking sad with," he said matter-of-factly. "Keep an eye on those fuckers. Make sure they aren't skimming any fucking cash or up to anything shady."

"OK, no problem, I'll keep an eye on them."

"Now come outside; the guys have been working on your car for you."

"Working on my car?" The mind boggled. What guys? Oil slicks, rockets and ejector seats whizzed through my head.

No such luck.

"We've installed a remote safe – here's the key fob for it. Just open your boot and press the key, and out it fucking pops." Terry pressed the key and out it fucking popped, a hidden door came out of the side of the boot. "So you can keep any cash safe; you can't be too careful, a lot of thieving fuckers around. Especially after those fucking pirates."

"Well, cool. I mean it's a bit Mexican drug cartel, but why not? Not quite the James Bond action I was hoping for – when do I get the ejector seat?" I asked.

"Maybe later," laughed Terry.

I jumped in the car, lit up a fag and waved Terry goodbye as I drove off. I flicked a glance at the first name and lay-by address on my clipboard. It was Arthur's old site; strangely, he'd quit a while back, just after the fire. A new chap had taken over his slot, another little Englander, retired, caravanning type. I'd met him briefly a few mornings before. Also, the pen scribble that read "caravanning motherfucker" next to his name was a bit of a giveaway. Terry's business notes were very helpful.

His name was Brian. I pulled in past the signs and the new board touting our Wimbledon Special. Brian was just waving goodbye to a coachload of Taiwanese tourists as I walked over to him. He seemed like he was in fairly good shape and spirits, and looked pretty young and sprightly for his age. His trousers gave him away, though – they were a dark green corduroy. He smiled as I walked towards him. I don't think he recognised me.

"Hi, strawberries and cream?" he offered.

"No thanks. I'm Adam; I work for Dave. He might have told you to expect me."

He was vaguely expecting me, and he looked genuinely pleased that I wasn't quite as daunting as Dave and Terry. That Terry's a big lad, he said a couple of times too many in the course of our chat. He was a fucking big lad, to be fair. I made small talk in between customers with him. We chatted about Wimbledon, how busy it was and how the specials were doing, and the downsides of storing a lot of cream in a freezer box.

We also, of course, discussed his love of caravanning. He was another confusing Eurosceptic who loved travelling in Europe, although he wasn't as full of hatred as some of the others. He even liked French food and didn't call it "foreign muck" which was a refreshing change. He had a strong penchant for a cheese called Maroilles, which he claimed both smelt and tasted of very dirty socks. I couldn't imagine how that could be a good thing, but he seemed adamant that I should try it. I half-expected him to whip some out of the corduroy trouser pocket. Despite his passion for cheese, he still hated Europeans as a whole and didn't trust them one bit.

"Had a coachload of bloody Germans earlier," he insisted on telling me.

I could imagine the Basil Fawlty scene which probably ensued. My initial surprise at how he didn't seem too bad soon subsided as he moved swiftly on to describe a "bunch of fucking Japanese tourists". Before he could tell me what they got up to and dig himself in any deeper, I gave him my mobile number and told him to call me if he had any problems with anything other than caravans or foreigners.

Off I went to the next name on my very long list. This one had a sad face scribbled in red marker pen next to it – one to watch, apparently. He was called John and was – if Terry's notes were anything to go by – a bit of a sneaky twat. I pulled up at the far end of the lay-by and figured I'd watch for a minute or two to see if anything nefarious appeared to be going on. I had no idea what that might be, of course. Stealing money? Stealing fruit? Selling a side-line of under-the-counter jam? I wonder what had been written next to my name. I'd certainly been helping myself to a lot of fruit initially.

I watched a family buying some Wimbledon Specials after their son had pissed all over the side of the lay-by. A coachload of tourists pulled up in between us and started getting out and stretching their legs. It was a bunch of hilarious elderly English types on a South West coach trip. They were always fun to watch – a much less organised and chaotic affair than any of the Asian coach parties.

In fact, it was like watching a slow-motion zombie ballet. They landed on the road with a groan; some ambled towards the fruit stall, some into the field and some towards me. A very worried-looking young tour manager armed with a clipboard, a whistle and a small orange flag darted in and out amongst them, trying to keep them all from straying too far. It was an endless, Herculean task – his best bet seemed to be to herd them towards the queue for strawberries, as at least that gave them some focus. A couple of them were making a break from the pack and had somehow managed to climb over the barbed wire fence into the field. They appeared to be interested in the sheep. The tour manager swore, put his clipboard down and sprang into action.

But a few steps and a brave leap over the barbed wire fence proved to be a naïve move on his part. The bottom of his trousers caught on the barbed wire and flung him down onto the grass. Thankfully he landed in a nice soft pile of sheep shit, which was great for the head trauma and terrible for the rest of the day on a hot coach.

I nearly spat my coffee out, I was laughing so hard.

He shouted something obscene at the old couple, who had unsurprisingly switched their interest from the sheep over to him. They were fussing over him like a long-lost grandchild, saying sorry endlessly and trying to clean him up with small pieces of tissue paper that the lady seemed to want to lick first. They were largely smearing the shit across him even more, but at least their heart was in the right place. He got them both over the fence and back on the coach and went and changed his shirt for a wisely packed spare —something like this must have happened before.

Anyway, I'd lost focus. I jumped out of the car and headed over to speak to John – he still had a small queue of coach stragglers patiently waiting and drooling. I walked up around the side and introduced myself. He seemed friendly enough – he was mid-thirties, very young for one of our team, with curly ginger hair and glasses. He looked, at worst, like he might think it was OK to take the odd tenner here and there. Not much way of telling, I guess, other than keeping a close eye on stock levels or spying on him somehow. Perhaps I could disguise myself as a hedge?

But disguises and petty cash thievery could wait for another day; I had a long list to get through.

I chatted to him about the weather – he said it was too fucking hot for gingers – and after a little moan about the stench of warm fruit, I headed onwards.

Over the next few hours, I covered about eighty miles, stopping to introduce myself to another fruit seller every few miles. It was remarkable how many there were. I never really noticed it until I started this job. It seemed like they were more of a thing about twenty years ago – I had some vague childhood memories of my dad stopping to buy me some cherries to stop me crying when I was very young. Like most of my childhood memories, I couldn't quite picture it clearly. It seemed like a memory of something I'd been told, rather than a real one. But actually, these stalls were everywhere. The 'Pret a Mangers' of rural England – you were never more than a few seconds from one.

The sellers all seemed busy. They all complained about the heat, and they mostly seemed to have caravans and wanted to talk about this fascinating aspect of their lives.

I arrived at the fifteenth lay-by (nearly halfway through my list) to check in with Toby, another sixty-something earning a bit of cash on the side. Where the fuck did Dave find them? Did he hang around bingo rooms, funerals and bakeries? God knows. As I pulled in, these thoughts vanished – there was a police car in front of the fruit stall, with a slightly worried-looking Toby shaking his head and pointing at the fruit. I parked up and quickly walked over to see what was going on.

"Hi, I'm Adam, Toby's manager. Anything I can do to help, officers?"

Toby looked relieved that someone had arrived to deal with this. "These gentlemen were asking if I had my license; otherwise, they'd have to stop me from selling and confiscate my fruit."

"Really?" I asked them.

"Yes, sir," said the taller of the two officers. "We need to see a copy of the trading license."

"OK, give me two seconds to call the boss."

"Yeah, you do that," said one of them in a surprisingly fast and squeaky voice.

I called Dave and explained the situation.

"Does one of them have big ears?" he asked.

I tried to casually look at their ears without making it super-obvious that I was trying to look at their ears. I noticed that one of them had a gigantic pair of lug holes on him.

"Yes."

"Does one of them have a voice like he's inhaled helium?"

I laughed. "Yes, actually exactly that."

"Fucking Charles and Camilla!" he said, laughing down the phone. "Give them fifty quid and tell them I said to fuck off."

"You want me to say that to them?"

"Yes, exactly that!"

I hung up, got my wallet out as discreetly as possible and popped £50 into a punnet of strawberries. I passed the strawberries over to the one with big ears.

"Dave said to give you this and to tell you to fuck off. So, fuck off!" I added for good measure.

Toby went red and looked like he might explode at any second. I think telling the police to 'fuck off' was too much for his brain to deal with. He suddenly resembled a pigeon that had been accidentally pecking at a discarded wrap of cocaine. His head pecked back and forth and his beady eyes stuck out like they wanted to escape.

"Fucking Dave, tell him to go screw himself," the policeman said, taking the strawberries and cash.

They both ate a strawberry, turned around and walked off towards their car, throwing the strawberry ends down with overzealous force. They threw the rest of the punnet into the hedge.

"See you soon," said the smaller-eared one, possibly trying to sound menacing and failing miserably. Sounding like a field mouse on helium can't make being in the police any easier, I thought. With that, they jumped in their car and sped off.

"That was weird," I said to Toby as if it was nothing. "Anyway, I'm Adam. Dave probably told you to expect me."

The rest of the chat went as all the others had; I even let him talk caravans for five minutes to distract him from what had just happened and hopefully help him forget all the talk of licenses. I'd gathered from Dave's happiness to give away £50 that we probably didn't have one. He enthusiastically informed me that his caravan was a shiny new one, with a fancy toilet and a power shower.

"Where does the shit go?" I asked him. I'd always been curious about this. Was it like a boat, and it just plopped out down below? Did trains do that too? Where did all the poo go?

"Well, I'm glad you asked that," he replied with a straight face. "It goes into a cartridge you can empty at the site."

"A cartridge? A cartridge of shit?" I could almost smell the 3D printing potential.

"Yes, it's about this big and is sealed, so it's all clean and hygienic."

"Yes, it sounds it." You learn something new every day. "Where do you put your cartridge when it's full?" My mind couldn't quite let it go.

"You empty it in a special area at the caravan park."

"Oh. Who empties the special area?"

"I never thought to ask," he replied.

I finished our fascinating excrement chat and sped off to the next couple of lay-bys. After working through the very long list, I was on my third-to-last stop of the day. I'd been whizzing through them at an increasing speed. But now, as the end was in sight, the fucking traffic was suddenly never-ending and never moving. I finally pulled over into the next lay-by.

Freddie (who had the honour of a smiley face next to his name) waved at me and walked over to my car. We'd met outside the warehouse a few days before, and he seemed like a nice old chap.

"Bloody roadworks, bet that took you an age to get up here?"

"Yes, but you must be doing well. Are you walking down the traffic jam queues?"

He looked at me like I'd lost my mind. "Walking the queue? I'm seventy-two. I'm not walking up and down in the sun all day."

"Fair enough." I hadn't thought of that problem. We needed some young blood. "How's the caravan?" I asked him, not remembering if he had one but assuming he probably did.

"Oh, it's wonderful. I just bought a new interior for it. Have I shown you the photos yet?"

"Oh yes, you did," I lied. "It looks amazing."

"Off to France with the missus, once this season is over."

"That'll be nice. Bring me back some French

saucisson."

"Oh no, we don't eat none of that foreign muck when we're over there, plays havoc with Deirdre's belly, that stuff does. Last time she didn't leave the caravan for a week."

"Did you get through a lot of cartridges?" I asked, trying out my new knowledge.

"Yes, they fucking stank. I dropped one on the way to the deposit point. Splattered all over my new trousers, it did."

"Well, thanks. That's an image I won't be getting out of my head for a while."

"No, me neither," he muttered as he turned and served a couple of Americans after some strawberries and directions to Stonehenge.

I held back from trying to explain to him that French food was no longer foreign when you were in France, it was just food. All the caravaners were the same – they loved to travel to France but were terrified of anything French. They refused to learn anything more than "bonjour" as a point of British pride in their own stupidity – only making the bi- or tri-lingual French person they were talking to hate them even more. If you are going to travel to Northern France, make sure you speak French well – or if you don't, then pretend you are German or Greek. Anything but British. If they spot you, you're in trouble. From raw burgers, roast beef name-calling to conversations about William the Conqueror, nothing is off-limits. It was a culture war, and it had been raging for hundreds of years.

You can't blame them, though – we're a horrible bunch of caravanning cunts and complaining red-faced idiots.

If they came here, they got the same, of course. From spat-on food, frog name-calling to conversations about Agincourt and endless, endless "saving their bacon in the war" comments.

I didn't say any of that, of course, and just finished chatting about caravan interior trends before I politely made my excuses and left. I hit the last two spots on the way back to the warehouse – two more old chaps and two more chats about caravans (well, one was a motorhome, if we're going to be specific).

Back at the warehouse, Dave was at his desk, and Terry was at another, with his back to us. Dave waved me over as he finished up a phone call.

"So, how was that?"

"Yeah, good, but I think we need to sort two things straight away. Firstly we need more roadworks so we can sell directly to the cars."

"You want me to conjure up some fucking roadworks? Terry, pass my magician's cape and hat," replied Dave, sounding like he might be regretting my promotion already. But then his face suddenly changed, and he looked like he was having a small epiphany. He flipped open a laptop and started typing.

"Can't we just blow up the road?" shouted Terry over the never-ending whirring noise of a money counter from the back of the room.

I laughed, imagining he was joking. They both looked at me with a puzzled look, indicating otherwise.

"I was thinking more along the lines of some fake traffic jams," I said. "Just putting up the lights and then fucking off for a few days. How would anyone know?"

"Oh right, yes, that sounds easier," shouted Terry. "Less explosives to deal with."

"Just what I was thinking," said Dave as he turned the laptop around and showed me an eBay search full of traffic cones and lights. "You might be onto something."

"Well, cool, but even if we get that sorted, there is problem number two."

"Do tell."

"Well, this army of old people you've somehow managed to employ is great and all, they give the whole thing a relaxed, local vibe. But they don't particularly want to be walking up and down a line of cars all day in the heat."

"They think it's neat," shouted a confused Terry.

"Heat, Terry, heat. The fucking sunshine, they hate it, and all the money comes from walking up and down the queues with the new specials. People who've been stuck in traffic for an hour can't be arsed to pull over afterwards. They just want to get out of there."

"We could try persuading them to walk up to the cars," added Terry menacingly.

"I think we might need an ambulance if we do that. What we need is a bunch more like that Keiron lad you sent me, but with a bit more hustle. They can walk up and down chatting to people, and the oldies can stay and prepare the fruit and serve anyone who walks up."

"OK, well, sounds like you need to do some recruiting

then. Go get some young people for us. I think me and Terry can get all the traffic gear we need without too many problems. I know a man who can sort us out," claimed Dave.

"I can probably get a bunch of students who want to earn some cash, if I go and spend the evening down the uni. No idea how good they will all be, but it'd be a start."

"OK, sounds like a fucking plan," said Dave happily. "I'll tell Gregg you're busy for tonight, and he can take his fucking brother. He's always asking me to give the useless fucker some work."

"Busy night then," said Terry as he finished whirring through his last bundle of cash.

"We need about ten plus young'uns for tomorrow. I reckon we'll be able to get enough traffic light kits to get about that many spots going. We can always add more later on," said Dave.

"I guess I'm off to campus then," I said as I stood up to leave.

With that, I headed down to the university to see if I could do some recruiting. Maybe I could bring a van by each morning and pick up a bunch of students for some cash-in-hand work. I suspect I'd need to offer some half-decent money and bonuses to get them onboard, but it was worth a try.

I spent about two hours chatting with about a hundred different students in a massive beer garden just inside the university grounds. I hadn't been near a campus for about a decade; they'd changed a lot. The once-crumbling old buildings had largely been replaced with shiny glass tributes to forward-thinking architecture. They'd age just as well as the old ones did, I suspected. The students were still pretty much the same, though. Different fashion, different drinks of choice and cigarettes had largely been replaced with vapes, but otherwise, much the same. Weirdly, some of the clothes that were in when I was at uni were being worn ironically now. I must be getting old.

I'd found fifteen people who were keen to start work tomorrow. It was about five more than I needed, but I figured at least a few would flake on me – it was an 8am start, after all. I'd hardly blame them; maybe the beer garden wasn't the perfect place for recruiting, thinking about it. But it was all done now.

I called Terry and arranged to borrow the minibus that he had knocking about at the warehouse.

That was a long first day as a fruit executive regional manager. Aha!

# CHAPTER 8

# ROADWORKS EVERYWHERE

The next day, I was down at the warehouse an hour before the staff, as requested by Terry at about three in the morning. Did he ever sleep?

It looked like there was a council construction conference going on, with dozens of people in hard hats and fluoro jackets milling around smoking fags and doing fuck-all. It was almost like they were real. We just needed a table with a tea urn to complete the picture.

Dave and Terry emerged with Hans, all dressed in site foreman outfits, clipboards and walkie-talkies in hand. They looked like they were off for a hard day on a building site shouting at people. I'm guessing they hadn't got any of this off eBay since Dave increasingly struck me as someone who didn't like to pay for things, and I'm not sure they did same-day delivery.

"All good then?" asked Dave. "You got the extra workers?"

"Yes, picking them up in a bit from the uni."

"OK, good, we're going to take this lot and get these lights set up." He gave a Dave-wave in the direction of a massive pile of traffic lights and signs tangled up in the back of a lorry.

I thought it best not to ask where they got it all from, and instead, let them get on with it. I grabbed the keys to the slightly rusty old minivan and went to optimistically pick up fifteen students from the front of the uni. When I got there, only four of them had made it and they looked a little hungover. We waited for ten minutes, and another three showed up. Well, seven wasn't too bad.

I took them to the nearest Starbucks and bought everyone double espressos; they looked like they needed it, and hopefully, it would perk them right up.

I went through the pay and bonuses in the Starbucks car park and what they had to do throughout the day. I told them there were a lot of roadworks and we were making double teams so someone could walk along and sell fruit to the cars. I didn't think they needed to know that we were the source of the roadworks. I explained how many I'd sold in just one day, and a few of their greedy little eyes lit up at the thought of the bonus, which was hopefully a good sign. Maybe they'd be alright.

We jumped into the mystery van, as they were affectionately calling it. Less because it looked like the now-even-more-ironically-trendy Scooby Doo van, more because it was a mystery how it started and hadn't killed us all. It emitted a massive plume of black smoke as the engine kicked in, straight into two businessmen armed with lattes and briefcases. The students all started laughing and filming them on their phones as they emerged from the cloud of dirty smoke. They looked less than happy.

Off we went.

We arrived at the first lay-by a few minutes later, and I dropped off the first slightly more awake new team member with Toby, who looked somewhat overwhelmed by his queue. I gave him a wave.

I dropped the rest of them off over the next hour and spun the trembling monster of metal around to head back to the warehouse. My phone had already started ringing with people needing refills. It seemed like Gregg was struggling to top-up all the teams quickly enough and they were selling out – especially the spots with new helpers and even newer roadworks. I sped around country lanes shouting at people on speakerphone that I was on the case and we'd have them topped up soon. I arrived at the warehouse and slammed on the dodgy brakes, only coming to a grinding halt a few inches short of the warehouse wall. The brakes seemed to be on their way out too. Fuck driving this every day.

I jumped out and ran over to the main door of the warehouse to see what was going on and why everyone was waiting for fruit. As I pulled one of the doors open a crack, a load of strawberries flew over my head and out onto the forecourt. I ducked down, avoiding most of them and entered the sticky mayhem that awaited inside. Dave was having a meltdown, he was screaming at a few of the unboxers and throwing fruit at anyone foolish enough to make eye contact. Gregg was standing at the back of the warehouse, looking nervous. No wonder all the refills weren't happening. I dodged around the side of Dave's rage and headed to the end of the warehouse and up the stairs to where Terry was.

"What's going on?" I asked him.

"Dave saw a couple of them eating his strawberries when we got back from setting the roadworks up. He hates it when people eat his fucking strawberries."

"My phone has been ringing nonstop, everyone needs refills, and Gregg can't get anywhere near the fruit because he's shitting himself over there in the corner," I said, pointing down at a nervous-looking Gregg.

"Shit, I hadn't even noticed him. What a lazy prick!" said Terry, already halfway down the stairs. He marched over to Gregg and grabbed him by his collar, dragging him to the other end of the warehouse. "Why the fuck are you standing about watching this? Get your fucking lazy arse out of here and do some fucking work."

Terry had gone an interesting shade of tomato.

They both started loading strawberries onto one of the shelves on wheels. I came down to give a hand and started unpacking more boxes of Aldi strawberries. Gregg looked a bit shaken up by the whole thing, I felt bad for him. Terry seemed like a bit of a cunt when he wanted to be.

Where did they get all these weird strawberries from, I wondered as I cut open another box and dumped the contents into a punnet. I'd never looked closely before, assuming that they got them on the day they were going off. I'd kidded myself that perhaps what we were doing was helping with food waste. But this fruit was still very much in date for another five days. I grabbed another container of plastic strawberry boxes and started tearing into them – they were all in date too. This wasn't quite the eco-friendly, locally sourced farm business I had always imagined it to be.

Dave's temper was going to cause us a big bottleneck. We needed a lot more strawberries, pronto. Between our mysteriously appearing roadworks and the additional student workers, levels were running low everywhere. Terry and Gregg rushed back in with an empty wobbling shelf on wheels. They loaded up the last of the strawberries, and Terry gave Gregg a push and told him to get a fucking move on.

"Gregg's all loaded up," Terry shouted. I went out to the yard and caught him before he vanished.

"Gregg, go and do the nearest lay-bys first. Everyone needs a top-up. I'll get on with the further away ones in a minute."

"OK, OK," said a flustered Gregg.

"Right, we need the team back and focused," I told Terry.

"Dave," Terry shouted at a mildly calmer Dave, who was still lecturing the team about his strawberries.

"What?" he snapped.

"We've got a backlog. Can they get back to work, please?"

"Sure, sure. No more stealing my fucking strawberries." He threw a last handful of strawberries at them as an exclamation mark. "Back to fucking work," he shouted and stomped off up the stairs to the office.

They rushed back to their tables and started ripping open boxes at double speed. Terry and I loaded up my car with as much fruit as we could, and I sped off to help with the top-ups. I flew around each lay-by, dropping off a quick fruit top-up for everyone, dodging down traffic jams with my indicators on, as if I was meant to be there. Fruit emergency! I should get a special flashing light; a big red glowing strawberry on top of my car would do it.

The roadworks were doing the trick; seven of our lay-bys had new traffic lights and building work signs with cones everywhere. Not a worker in sight of course, so nothing seemed out of place. British holidaymakers would undoubtedly feel unnerved if they made it to their destination without coming across at least a few sets of unmanned roadworks or a lengthy diversion. It's like they waited for the hottest days to fix holes – or in this case, it was like a bunch of fruit sellers had set up loads of fake roadworks to sell more fruit. Both scenarios seemed equally ridiculous.

Business was going well, and the sales were crazy everywhere I went. I dropped off the last of my strawberries and headed back to the warehouse for more. It was eerily calm when I arrived; Dave stalked amongst the tables of fruit unpackers like the angel of death. He muttered to himself as he walked, standing and staring menacingly at anyone who dared look up at him. Terry loaded up more fruit into my car, popped a couple of freezer bags full of cream on my front seat, and I was off again. As I left, Gregg pulled into the car park for another top-up.

"Fucking crazy out there," he said to me as he got out, and I sped off.

The first drop-off was to a chap called Nigel, who was working with Tony, his new student helper. I passed them over a load more boxes of strawberries.

"Busy today," said Nigel.

"Yeah, it's Wimbledon, always hectic."

"Yes, I'm listening now," he said, pointing to a battered old radio on the table. Wimbledon didn't translate to the radio that well – about on a level with golf – and listening next to a traffic jam surely didn't help. I could just hear the occasional round of polite applause.

"Who's winning?"

"God knows, I can't hear a thing. Can I give you some cash, please? It's making me a bit nervous," he said.

"Yeah, sure. I think Terry is running behind with collections today."

He passed me over a big wad of cash which I stuffed in my pocket.

"Should be about two thousand there."

The same thing happened at the next three stops. The old chaps were getting a bit jittery, holding two or three grand in their pockets. It was more than they normally took in two days.

I had about twelve grand on me by the time I returned to the warehouse. I could see now why they fitted my car with the safe from mexicandruglords.com. All the cash was in it, just in case I got held up by fruit pirates or a fruit-fancying highwayman – 'Stand and deliver, your fruit or your life.'

I pulled in around the side of the warehouse, opened the car safe, took out the bag full of cash and headed into the office. Dave wasn't there; he was apparently still pacing around the warehouse, keeping the team of terrified fruit unpackers in line. Terry was behind the desk with a money counter, and Hans was putting piles of counted money into big black canvas barrel bags. I went over and emptied my bag into the pile on the desk.

"Good day?"

"Not bad," said Terry, not even looking up from the counting machine, which was whirring away as he stacked it with endless piles of cash. It looked like the montage scene from a drug-dealing film — the bit when all is good and all the money is flowing in. Normally followed by men with moustaches walking into a bank to pass over their ill-gotten bags full of money to the happy-looking bankers. They were happy because they usually seemed to end up keeping it all. That bit was always confusing to me — if you can't handle a banker, don't become a drug lord.

"Can you go and collect cash off this list, please, Adam? I'm a bit snowed under. They keep calling me." Terry pushed a list towards me with one hand as he loaded more notes with the other.

"Yeah, sure, I'll do it when I drop some more fruit off. It's mayhem out there today."

"Yes, it is your fucking strawberry and cream / traffic jam combination," Hans said.

"I might have to ask for another pay rise," I half-joked.

I wasn't even sure how much I was meant to be getting paid now, so I guess that might be a little pre-emptive. Time and, knowing Dave, a suspicious brown envelope of cash would tell.

I flew around ten lay-bys, grabbing increasingly large piles of cash: £2500, £3000, £3600. I was struggling to close my safe as I put the money in from the last collection. God knows how much was in there, but it was a lot. I was all out of fruit again too.

I got back to the warehouse and found Terry just finishing off the last pile of money and lighting up a fag to celebrate. He didn't look happy to see me.

Hans was relaxing by the coffee machine with a fresh espresso in his hand, making another for Terry.

"Fuck's sake, I only just finished."

"Sorry," I said as I dumped two Co-Op bags of money in front of him. I'd put each person's cash pile in an envelope with their name on it so I didn't have to count it on the road.

"I think Gregg should have the last top-ups in hand, so I can help if you want?"

"OK, good." He wrote down the name of each bag and then ripped it open and dumped it on the table.

"Sort this pile into different note types and then pass them to me and let's get this cash out of here." We all dived into the dirty, fruit-stained pile of notes spilling off the table. After an hour of silent money piling, folding and stacking later, it was all done and loaded into four large bags.

"Right then, grab a fucking bag and let's get this out of here," Terry said.

We both picked up the bags and headed for the door. Terry stopped to grab something out of Dave's top drawer on the way. We loaded the bags into the back of his Range Rover, and he threw a blanket over them (that'll fool them). We all jumped in and headed out of the estate.

I wondered where we were going – the bank? Surely not. Where do you stash four large bags of cash from semi-legal fruit sales? Maybe we were going to bury it somewhere. A ten-minute drive later and I realised how wrong I was. We were, in fact, just dropping it off at the local bank – or banks, to be more precise. We pulled up next to a Lloyds, which was over the road from a Barclays. Terry handed me a bag and a paying-in book.

"You do Lloyds then; everything is completed for you. Hans, go with him."

He jumped out with one of the other bags.

"Back here in five."

I walked into Lloyds with the bag over my shoulder and a strange German shadow behind me. I felt like I was about to rob the place, but in reverse – the Robin Hood of banking. I robbed the poor and gave to the banks. The poor darlings have had a tough time since the recession. They'd even put a limit on their bonuses – it was criminal, really.

It felt like everyone was looking at me – they weren't, of course, but a bag full of money makes you feel pretty paranoid. I sweated my way to the start of the queue; my legs felt like somebody else was controlling them. I waited my turn in a line full of old people and local business types: Shelley from the hairdressers, Tim from WHSmith and Edna, who'd come to get her pension; I imagined that's who they were anyway. The one in front of me looked like an Edna. She was all varicose veins and cardigans. No wonder banks were all shutting their branches down. Nobody came apart from businesses and old people, and I'm pretty confident the old people weren't bringing in the big money.

I got to the front after Edna had enlightened the cashier about her hip playing up. A large spectacled lady summoned me over.

"Hi, here for a deposit, er, to make a deposit," I stammered. I pushed the book over to her.

"OK, thank you," she said as if nothing weird was going on.

She opened the book and must have been surprised by the amount at the exact moment that I dumped the heavy bag of money onto the counter. The unzipping noise the bag made broke the tension.

"I might just grab another money counter," she said, looking a little flustered.

"Yes, probably best; otherwise, we might be here for a while."

She made her way off to an office behind her to grab one, and I took the opportunity to start unloading bricks of notes onto the counter. Now everybody was looking at me – it wasn't paranoia this time. An enormous pile of money will do that, even in a bank.

The woman returned and plugged in another money counter. She gave me a glance over the growing pile of cash.

"OK," she said as she grabbed the first pile, split the band and put it into the two counters. It whizzed through in no time, and she put a new paper band around it, which she scribbled on and moved on to the next one. I finished emptying the bag onto the counter and zipped it back up, slinging it over my shoulder. Hans was no help at all and just stood behind me, looking suspicious.

I weirdly felt a bit less sweaty and odd since I'd put the money on the counter. I don't know what I was expecting; I was just depositing money for a business, nothing to see here, albeit a slightly dodgy business that bribed the odd policeman and had the odd gun fight, but a business nonetheless.

I shuffled the pile of money around, pretending to be in some way useful at this point in the proceedings. She whirled her way through the piles at top speed with her two machines, typing everything into a calculator as she went. We were soon done; she stamped the paying-in book and printed off a paying-in slip.

"Here you go," she said.

"Is he with you?" She asked, nodding at Hans.

"Yes, sorry about him." I apologised. "Thanks, that was very quick. Have a good day."

I made my way out with Hans still following and back to the Range Rover. Terry was already back and waiting inside. He'd even managed to get a coffee.

"All good?"

"Felt a bit weird, but yes, fine."

With that, we sped off to the next two banks to drop off the last two bags. I didn't ask why we had to go to four banks if it was just a legit business paying their takings in. But I'm sure there was probably a great reason for it, I thought to myself as I returned from paying £95,000 into NatWest. Once it was all done, we grabbed another quick coffee and headed back to the warehouse.

We spent a few hours helping to tidy up the mess from Dave's earlier fruit outburst. There were strawberries and fruit splatters everywhere; we hosed it all down and swept it out into the courtyard and down the drain.

"Dave love to throw fruit," Hans whispered.

"Yes, he does seem to. Is he always like that?"

"Yes, all the time I know him," he replied.

"Doesn't it bother you? I mean, he calls you Hans the German."

"Yes, he does. I don't care," he laughed "he loves the old England. The Empire."

"What like in Star Wars?" I asked giving away my love of films over history.

"No. Not Star Wars. The British Empire."

"Oh, that Empire. Well, that explains a few things." I chuckled.

Dave appeared from the top office with a coffee in his hand; he shouted at me from the top of the stairs.

"You're in late tomorrow, Adam, about six, late-night shift, dress warm." With that, he disappeared back into his office.

"What's that all about?" I asked Terry.

"Special mission tomorrow night, you'll see. Good work today."

I was none the wiser; I'd almost given up asking. I headed home.

# CHAPTER 9

# NICE DAY OFF?

The next day I woke up late and lounged around the house for the afternoon; Wimbledon was on in the background, and the doors were open. I sat in the garden for a bit and enjoyed a coffee, a spliff and some sunshine. It was nice not to have to deal with any fruit while it was sunny. I really must sort out this house. Perhaps I should start with the garden. Thankfully, there was a small stone patio area next to the doors, which wasn't yet too overgrown for me to sit on. The rest was a bit of a right-off. It looked like there were about ten metres of garden running back towards the open fields at the end. But it was totally overgrown and had gone wild. Maybe I'd go and get a strimmer. Fuck it. I was off and on my way to B&Q before I could talk myself out of it.

I entered the gigantic warehouse and was immediately overwhelmed by my lack of man skills and knowledge. I headed for the garden tool section and picked what looked like an okay-ish strimmer. By okay, I mean it wasn't the cheapest, which would obviously be shit, but it wasn't too expensive either. After all, what the fuck did I know about strummers. I picked the strimmer up, paid and headed home, resisting the urge for a fried burger of doom from the filth wagon outside. The onions made it smell better than it was, no doubt.

Once home, I made a coffee and plugged in the strimmer. It all looked simple enough. After an exhausting twenty minutes of strimming, I had broken the strimming cord about ten times and gave up. Tiring business, gardening. I wondered how gardeners do this shit all day.

After a couple more coffees and an unbelievably bad cheese toastie, it was just about time to head off. What a very productive day off, I thought, looking at the tiny area of cleared garden with a feeling of slightly pathetic male pride. I stuck a torch, a beanie and some gloves into a bag. Grabbed a jacket and headed out the door, ready for whatever the night would bring.

I got to the warehouse, Terry and Gregg were slouching on fruit packing tables, smoking fags and drinking Starbucks coffees. Terry fucking loved Starbucks. I'd barely seen one out of his hand; he blamed it on Wimbledon, saying he needed the extra motivation to get through the busy period.

"Alright, lad, nice day off?" he asked.

"Yeah, not bad. I did a bit of gardening, actually."

"Get fucking Titchmarsh over here," he said to Gregg. "Right, we're off to grab some extra stock, seeing as your Wimbledon Specials have been getting through our regular supplies so quickly."

"Fair enough."

We walked out on the main road, locking up the

warehouse as we left; Terry locked the metal gates with a big thick chain and padlock and waved us over to a lorry parked at the side of the road.

He chucked the keys to Gregg. "You're driving."

"OK, I drive," said Gregg. Thank God for that. I didn't fancy driving this beast around.

We all jumped in, and he started it up. Terry pressed a few buttons on the sat-nav until it chirped up. Turn left in a hundred yards, she suggested to us. We set off; I wondered where we were off to – maybe one of those massive markets over by Essex that sells fish at two in the morning. There must be one for fruit too.

Terry turned the stereo up, and "Ghost Town" blared out of the tinny, cheap-sounding speakers as we trundled down the deserted country lanes on our way to who knows where.

"How long have you been over here, mate?" I asked Gregg.

"About seven years now."

"Always around here?"

"Yes, always here. Dave gave me job when I arrive, so I stay."

"What did you do before?"

"I drive lorry for the electrical company."

"OK nice, well, I feel safer already. You weren't tempted to go back home after Brexit, then?"

"Fuck that. I hate it at home. England is home now. Dave did paperwork for me, so I can work."

"Well, that was nice of him." That seemed uncharacteristically nice of Dave. But then, maybe if he was going to lose a good worker, he'd go the extra mile.

Terry turned the stereo up even louder, which I took as a hint to shut the fuck up.

Forty minutes later, we turned onto a dual carriageway and headed north. I guess we weren't going to Essex.

"Where are we going?" I asked Terry.

"You'll see," he offered helpfully, "nearly there."

The lady that lived in the sat-nav told us to turn off, and we did, going down a country lane – who were we to ever doubt her?

"Slow down," Terry said to Gregg and turned the stereo off; he was staring at Google Maps on his phone, checking for something. "Here you go, pull in at this lay-by."

We pulled over into yet another pothole-ridden lay-by. These guys were obsessed with them.

Gregg parked up behind a large Sainsbury's lorry. Terry jumped out and told us to wait, a man appeared from the side of the lorry. He looked nervous and was drawing heavily on a cigarette. They shook hands, and Terry handed him an envelope which he flicked through before they both moved to the back of the lorry and started opening it up. It was, I suppose not surprisingly, full of strawberries.

He waved us both out, and we jumped out and came around to the open door; Terry was in the back of the lorry and dumped a box of strawberries into my arms.

"OK, let's go, stick these in the lorry."

We started loading boxes of strawberries around the side of the lorry and into ours. The stench was disgusting.

Sweet and sticky, there was leaking strawberry juice everywhere on the lorry floor.

Occasionally a car would come past, and we'd all have to try to hide or close the doors, so it didn't look too dodgy. I didn't want to question Terry's technique, but I thought the sight of a load of people legging it behind a lorry made us look more suspicious, but hopefully, nobody noticed.

About ninety exhausting minutes later, it was all loaded. Terry thanked the slightly less nervous-looking man as he locked up. Once he had gone, we headed off too.

"Well, that's not the fruit market I thought we were going to."

Terry laughed. "Who said anything about a market?"

"Well, I just imagined that was where the fruit might come from."

"It comes from all over," Terry explained. "It's early yet; more to go."

We headed back to the warehouse, unloaded and headed out again. My last illusion about this business had been shattered. The fruit was all dodgy, hooky, snide. I thought, just for a second at the start of this job, that maybe it was just end-of-date fruit or bulk-bought from somewhere. But no, it was all as dodgy as those fucking horrible cigarettes, that some shifty cunt was always trying to sell you down the pub.

We headed off in a Cornwall kind of direction. It was like a magical mystery tour of fruit crime. I wondered if Gregg had a real license to drive lorries. It seemed a little doubtful based on his somewhat erratic driving skills, but he seemed happy enough, so I suppose it was all good.

We pulled into a farm a few minutes later, bumping our way around a few courtyards to a couple of barns with some big silver storage silos. There was a grumpy-looking chap with a funny hat and a stick waiting with a couple of dogs. We pulled over, and Terry and I got out.

"Bout fuckin time, thought we said nine?"

"No, we said ten; you kept saying nine; you know it was ten," replied Terry curtly.

"I told you to leave that fucking Eastern European cunt behind this time, my dogs don't like the smell of him much." He pointed up at Gregg, who had remained in the lorry.

"This is Adam. You'll like him, he's very English," said Terry.

He shook my hand. I wasn't sure if that was meant to be an insult. What did very English mean?

"Nice to meet you," he said. I didn't bother replying, he seemed like a racist twat.

"Dave says fuck off, by the way," said Terry, interrupting the awkward silence I'd left hanging where my reply should have been.

"Of course he fuckin' did, fuckin' twat. You got my cash?"

Terry handed over a large envelope and the farmer waved us over to one of the barns. He slid open the large doors and told us to start loading. There were plastic bottles full of cream everywhere. They were loaded up in boxes and all over the floor. Cream everywhere. It fucking stank, an off-milk sweet smell that was like nothing I'd ever experienced. I gagged. Gregg emerged and we started loading up the boxes full of bottles into the back of the lorry. It was a stinking, creamy mess, even worse than the off-fruit smell I normally had to deal with.

Terry was chatting to the farmer and smoking a fag the whole time we were loading up. I'd have to start carrying some of those fetching swimming nose plugs. We finished loading the last few and secured the cream into the lorry. Terry shook hands with the farmer.

His dogs came over to say hi. Gregg looked instantly nervous and started backing off towards the lorry that he quickly jumped into. I gave them a quick stroke; they mostly seemed to want to lick the cream off my hands. Do dogs eat cream? These two did, but I guess they were Labradors, and Labradors eat everything. Gregg must have thought that included him.

"Tell Dave to fuck off," he shouted at our dust.

"Not a big dog fan then, mate?" I asked Gregg.

"No, a dog bite me when I was young." He proudly rolled up his sleeve to show me a big scar on his arm. "Go right through, big fucking dog!"

"Shit, that looks nasty; no wonder you don't like them."

"They all seem very nice," he added apologetically. "The farmer is wanker, though," he said.

We all agreed he was a wanker.

"You want to be scared of the farmer and not the dogs. I think he's much more likely to bite you than they are." Terry added.

"Yes, he not like me. Why is that?"

"Because you're a cunt," Terry replied helpfully.

"I think it's because he's a racist old prick," I interrupted.

"Yes, to be fair, he is a racist old prick. Don't mind him, Gregg," Terry answered, almost sounding compassionate for a second.

The next stop was just a few miles down the road. I recognised the sign; it was a massive Pick Your Own farm that everyone went to locally. We pulled in through the front gates, and a large farmer's-wife type with ruddy cheeks closed the gate behind us. She was wearing a Barbour and wellies and looked like she probably knew her way around a Sunday roast. She was the spitting image of the wife out of *The Darling Buds of May*, and I imagined she'd probably slaughtered and eaten a few pigs and a cow already today.

The place had a large concrete forecourt and a small kiosk for weighing your fruit and veg after you'd picked it. There was also a cute little 'wooden shack" style shop selling jam and other country crap, pickles and the like. It was a very popular place – during a weekend in the summer, the place was always packed. It was an amazing business model; they should make all farming like this. Who needs an army of vegetable pickers when people will pay to come and pick it themselves? As great a hustle as deconstructed "subscription box" meals and flat-pack furniture. Genius!

We all jumped out of the van.

"Alright, my lovely," she said, giving Terry's cheek an

enthusiastic squeeze between her two pudgy fingers. He looked terrified for the first time since I'd met him.

"How's Dave?" she asked while beckoning us over to a large pile of boxes.

"He's good, usual self," said Terry nervously.

"Good, my love. Well, you know what to do."

We all started grabbing the boxes of strawberries and loading them into the lorry. It didn't take long, as they were in large open boxes rather than endless smaller mini pallets that the supermarkets used. These were just massive boxes of slightly squishy fruit. We filled up the lorry with about fifty of them and then a couple of big boxes of cherries, too, for the odd person who still fancied a punnet.

"Can you boys give us a quick hand with the gate before you go?" the woman asked as we put the last box in the lorry.

"Yeah, of course, I'll sort the cash out for you. Adam will help you."

We walked over to the gate, and she passed me a crowbar.

"Make it look good," she said.

"What do you mean?" I asked.

"Break the lock and make it look good."

"Oh, I see. Insurance?"

"Yes, that's the one, love."

I jammed the crowbar into the chain that was wrapped around the gate; after a few seconds of pressure, the padlock pinged open and flew onto the floor.

"There you go."

"You've done that before, haven't you?"

I hadn't.

"Beginner's luck?"

I went to pass her back the crowbar.

"Can you do the office as well, please, dear?"

"I guess so, why not?"

We walked over to a wooden cabin, and she pointed at the door. I jammed the crowbar in near the lock and gave it a big push. It took a minute of pushing it back and forth before the wooden frame started to crack and then splintered.

"Lovely job, well done."

She gave the door a good kick, and it flew in. She seemed very happy with this and grabbed the crowbar off me. We both headed back over to Terry and Gregg. They were smoking fags at the front of our lorry. Terry looked eager to leave.

"All done?" Terry asked.

"Yes, my lovely, all done. Your new lad's got special skills. Very quick he was."

Terry passed her an envelope of money, and we jumped in to head off. She headed back to the office and started smashing the place up. I could see her grinning maniacally as pieces of wood flew everywhere. We pulled through the broken gates and back out onto the road.

"Well, you'll be pleased to hear that's it for today," said Terry once we were on the road. We headed back to the warehouse to unload; the cream was disgusting and stank of bad milk.

We hosed it down and loaded it into the fridge before

hosing down the lorry. Everywhere stunk of cream. It was almost enough to put Terry off his hundredth latte of the day, but not quite.

We parked the lorry outside on the road and locked up the warehouse. It was 4am by the time we finished, and I headed straight home as I had to be back in for 8am.

As I drove home through the deserted streets, I wondered (not for the first time) if I had made the right life choice with this job. Just when I thought I was out, they pulled me back in. Was that from *The Sopranos* or *The Godfather*? I couldn't remember, but it seemed relevant. Who would have imagined that selling strawberries would involve so much criminal activity? My attempt at a normal life was clearly flawed. But maybe I was overthinking the whole thing. It was hardly the mafia.

A bit of dodgy fruit never hurt anyone, did it?

# CHAPTER 10

# EXPANSION

Three hours of sleep later, I was up and showered and had joined Terry's world by drinking about ten coffees before I set off. Feeling slightly jittery and more than a little on edge, I pulled into the warehouse. The usual buzz of morning Wimbledon activity was afoot. The fruit unpacking from our fresh Sainsbury's boxes all seemed to be moving along as normally as possible. Maybe today would be a nice quiet one. I headed up the clanking metal stairs to the office.

Dave and Terry were waiting inside; Dave had a big map of the South of England that he'd pinned to a wall. Perhaps he was planning an invasion, I thought as I sat down.

"Right," he said, "we've been thinking about expanding. Here is where we're at currently." He'd put a load of tiny strawberry stickers at all the lay-by locations. As usual, the comedy seemed completely lost on Dave and Terry.

Dave grabbed a pack of small green pins from the table.

"These are the ones that are currently empty, that we

think might be good spots." He stuck about a dozen green pins on some roads around the Devon area.

I was amazed that Dave's love of war movies and documentaries hadn't manifested itself as a map on a table with little models of fruit being pushed around with long sticks. If I were the kind of person who bought their boss gifts, I'd get him a "War Room" sign for the office door.

"And then there is a load over here which might require a slightly more hostile takeover approach." He stuck bright pink pins in about fifteen locations around the New Forest area. "These are the big money ones that we need to focus on first."

"Now we've got to act fucking quick. Wimbledon's nearly over, and before you know it, the summer season will be over."

"Well, there's always the doubles?" I said.

"Nobody cares about the fucking doubles," laughed Terry.

"And what about over here?" I waved generally over a Cornwall and Devon kind of area.

"That's where those fucking nutter pirates are from. Maybe one day we'll deal with them properly."

"Too much of a bloody headache, that lot," Terry added.

"These are the best areas; we've got friends nearby, they are high profit, a longer season and the current owners have other, shall we say, financial interests which they care more about than fruit. So hopefully, they won't give a shit. We're going to do this today. No time like the present and all that.

"Oh, and remember what happened a few years ago? I don't want a repeat of that shit." Dave was looking at Terry when he spoke.

"They might have other interests, but surely they are going to put up a fight," added Terry.

"Don't get your knickers in a twist. Go and pick up some of the lads from over at the barracks. They've all got a few days' leave and have agreed to come and act like fruit sellers for us to help smooth the transition."

Terry looked relieved. "That'll do it."

"It fucking better, costing me a fortune; they put their freelance prices up again. They claim the army is cracking down on this kind of shit, although they might just be hustling me. I got us a new minibus, take that and fuck off!"

With that, Dave chucked Terry the keys.

We walked around the back of the warehouse to find a new (ish) white ten-seater mini-van looking considerably less death-trappy than the last one. On the back seats were a load of signs, hammers, drills and a few baseball bats for good measure. I wasn't sure they'd be all that useful for putting the signs up, but no doubt Terry would give it a go.

We headed off.

Forty minutes later, we pulled into a small town just above the A303. Despite masquerading as a normal town, it was actually a massive army barracks for the Salisbury Plain army training area. There were shooting ranges, 'Tank crossing' signs and all sorts of weirdness, along with more barbed wire fences than Australia during a rabbit outbreak. The place gave me the creeps. It was a glimpse of a possible Orwellian future; military police cars zoomed past us, cameras whirred and spun around to follow us.

We drove past the main entrance to the barracks and pulled in at a strange little diner at the side of the road. It looked like it had got lost in the Costa del Sol in the 80s. It was tired-looking and dated, with peeling window frames and filthy white walls. It had an enormous conservatory plonked onto one end, with a couple of smashed window panes to complete the look. As we pulled in, ten big-looking geezers were waiting in the car park.

Terry pulled over and jumped out, and they all started man-hugging each other. Clearly, they knew each other well. Terry didn't normally do that much hugging as a rule, but he seemed happy to make an exception for them. They must have all been in the forces together. It would certainly explain a few things.

Overly friendly greetings done, they all jumped in the minivan, and we sped off towards the New Forest.

Terry explained to them what was going on. He seemed more willing to communicate clearly with these guys; maybe he wasn't quite ready to trust me yet. He told me to fuck off whenever I asked him for any details.

It turned out that a few years ago, Dave had tried to expand his fruit-selling operations down to some of the very popular tourist lay-bys in the New Forest. It hadn't gone brilliantly, and a few of the stall holders had been given a bit of a kicking by the local crew. They were called the commoners. They build them a little strange in the

New Forest; it was all a bit of a "you aren't from around these ways and don't stray from the path" kind of vibe.

I'd gone on holiday there with my parents years ago, and my dad got in a fight with some of them. I'd never seen him in a fight before and wouldn't again. We were staying in a little bed and breakfast in a small village when our car alarm started going off at one in the morning. He went down and found a couple of pissed-up locals, jumping up and down on the car's roof. My mum and I watched the whole thing from our window.

Despite the dents in the roof, he was incredibly polite and asked them to "please get off", which they did. But then they started prodding him in the chest and telling him they could do what they wanted. He asked them to stop. They didn't. After about the tenth poke, he lost his cool. I didn't know he could fight until then. I'm not sure he did, either. He knocked the first one clean off his feet with an uppercut that came from nowhere. The second one got a drunkenly, half-arsed punch in, which seemed to stun him for a second. I can remember my mum's scream to this day; she'd have leapt out of the window to defend him if I hadn't been there.

By this point, the bed and breakfast owner had come out in his slippers and given the two lads a slap around the face, telling them he'd be in touch with their parents in the morning and they'd be paying for any damage. They soon fucked off. The old owner couldn't have been more apologetic. While plying my dad with free drinks, he explained that they were a pair of local commoners and were always causing *mischief*. I distinctly remember the use of that word to this day.

The commoners were a bunch of strange locals who looked after the land and the animals. They had been around for a long time, since around the 1200s. The whole thing centred around a couple of large land-owning families; with the land came certain rights. They were everywhere in the New Forest, like a network of spies – they'd infiltrated every local business and tourist attraction. They had certain rights over where they could go and the things they could do. The things they liked to do the most these days were deal drugs, sell fruit in lay-bys and extort money from tourists. They used most of the money to look after the land and all the free-roaming animals upon it, meaning everyone largely turned a blind eye. They all really fucking loved animals down there, so who cares about some drugs and unhappy tourists?

"One of my friends' daughters got sold some dodgy pills by them a few years back," Terry told his army friends. "She was only fifteen, and one of their boys sold some to her and her friends for a party. They all got pilled up in the middle of the forest. They got split up and started freaking out on these heavy, trippy pills. She got lost and was found half-alive the next day by the police. She claimed one of the commoners had attacked her when she asked for help in the woods."

"Fucking right horrible bunch of cunts," one of the army lads said. Terry's story had done the trick. I wasn't entirely sure how true it all was, but it seemed to have the desired effect and had worked them up into a killing frenzy.

135

Before long, we were at the first lay-by. We unpacked the first stall and dropped off two of the army guys. One was selling fruit, and the other was lurking (as someone from the army only can) in a hedge nearby, probably wearing camo. Hopefully, they wouldn't have to wait too long for some action as the sight of a pair of eyes staring at you from a hedge while you tried to buy strawberries might be slightly off-putting. Within thirty minutes, we had dropped them all off and set them up with military efficiency. Terry pulled over in the next lay-by.

"Right, this is us – you didn't think you were getting off that lightly, did you?"

We unloaded the last stall and signs and started setting up, hammering a couple of Wimbledon Specials signs in. We had a queue in no time. Terry, never one for customer interaction, decided to prowl around in the background, keeping an eye out for incoming trouble, while I doled out endless pots of strawberries and cream. The queue was ridiculous, and we were getting a slightly different crowd here, too. It's weird how different areas attract different types of tourists. This lot was heavy on the gammon, whereas back home, that was more true of the locals, not the tourists. Half the people stopping down here were exactly the people we had selling fruit at home – red-faced, unfit, retired caravaners. They were on their hols, and nothing was going to ruin it, except possibly a heart attack from ranting about bloody foreigners and lazy young people.

The rest of the customers were mostly families with well-spoken young children and immaculately behaved dogs. There was a noticeable absence of large coaches full of tourists – they clearly had no interest in the New Forest.

It didn't take long before there was a fruit buyer in the queue who looked a little out of place. The moment I saw him, I gave Terry a quick nudge. We'd all been waiting for the first one. Having just checked in with the rest of the teams, nobody had shown their face yet. At first, it was just one guy at the back of the queue; he was tall and skinny and had a slight mullet and goatee combination going on. You could always spot these guys from their facial hair and weird clothing, I'd learned from Dave when he was discussing our takeover of the area. He'd flipped the page over on a white chart he'd been scribbling all over. On the next page was a picture of what I, at the time, assumed was a character from *Emmerdale*, circa 1995. A Dingle of some kind. But no, it was what, in his mind, a commoner looked like. To be fair, he wasn't too far off.

The guy was wearing a tight old denim jacket and a deerstalker hat and looked like he had something suspicious concealed inside the jacket that he was keeping one arm over. He was joined after a few minutes by a fat, shorter chap with a very substantial moustache; it was big, bushy and somewhat Gallic in style. It was hard to see anything else. He joined his friend in the queue just as he was nearing the front.

Before them, I had to deal with a pair of out-of-place German tourists, something of a rarity. They were confused by the concept of strawberries with cream and wanted to know where the witches lived – I had no idea

137

what they were talking about on either count, but they were very persistent. I couldn't pay attention to what they were saying with two, bristly lunatics eyeballing me over their shoulders.

"Where are the witches, the witches!" they kept saying.

I gave up. "Oh yes, sorry. The witches. It's your accent. Go down the road for two miles, turn left, you can't miss it," I lied. That did the trick, and they fucked off.

Next in line were the pair of shifty-looking yokel types.

"Strawberries and cream?" I asked politely, making my way around the back of the stall to where I had stashed a baseball bat.

"No fucking strawberries, you fucking cunt. We told you lot before; this is our patch, we sell here."

"Sorry, I don't know what you mean," I said, even more politely than before. "I'm just selling fruit for my boss."

The taller one opened his jacket and let a small crowbar drop into his hand. I saw it coming a mile off; he wasn't the quickest cat in the cattery. Luckily it wasn't coming in my direction, so I just stood there watching. He took out a row of strawberry punnets in one savage swipe.

"I'm not going to fucking tell you again, you fucking prick," he shouted.

I stepped back and grabbed my baseball bat, swinging it towards the tall mulleted inbred. It hit the fruit-smashing streak of piss's hand, sending the crowbar clattering across the road. Terry, who had somehow gone unnoticed by the pair, flew in from the sidelines. His gigantic fist hit the shorter one right on the moustache.

The force sent him sprawling out into the road. If this was a 'come test your strength machine' at a fairground, then the bell was ringing, and Terry was collecting a goldfish in a bag. He jumped on top of him and continued to address his face with a flurry of fists. I walked round the stall towards Mr Deerstalker, who suddenly looked less cocksure.

"Consider us told," I shouted at him over the screaming noise of the rest of the queue as they fled in terror.

I jumped forward and went to fake-hit him; he scurried back into the hedges. He picked himself up and ran off up the lay-by, I turned around to check Terry hadn't gotten too carried away with the other one.

He had the man by the moustache and was violently shaking his head from side to side, trying to pull it off his face. Perhaps he thought it was fake and had taken offence. I pulled him off the bloody half-moustached mess. I grabbed the man by the ankles while he was down and dragged him a few feet out of the road. I didn't want him getting run over – that seemed a little excessive. He slowly crawled off up the lay-by away from us and towards his cowering friend, with a swift kick up the arse from me for good measure.

Terry's phone rang. "All good?" he said, panting.

I started to clear up the fruit mess from the road while he talked and paced around.

I splashed some water over the bloody road to get rid of anything that might deter the customers. There was a tuft of sad-looking moustache blowing around in the wind. The customers were back in no time – it took about two seconds for another car to pull in as if nothing had happened. The two fruit gangsters were sheepishly getting into their car and looked like they were going to fuck off for good.

Terry got off the phone and, in between customers, told me that two of the other lay-bys had just had similar incidents, and other than a few bruised fruits, it was three-nil so far to us. We had taken them by surprise while they were taking us by surprise. The others hadn't had anyone pay them a visit yet, but maybe they heard what was happening and had a rethink. If they came back, it probably wouldn't be today, and they'd definitely be more tooled up the next time.

"A fucking crowbar," chuckled Terry to himself.

The rest of the day was the usual blur of fruit, cream and customers. I was intrigued by how Terry and Dave had got into this fruit business and couldn't resist asking. Terry was surprisingly forthcoming – I think he was in a good mood after the fight. As I'd suspected, Dave and Terry had been in the army together. Dave had been Terry's Sergeant, in charge of his troop. They'd served in Afghanistan and Iraq together, along with half the guys from the barracks. Dave had left the army after injuring his foot. He told everyone who asked that it was some shrapnel from an explosion, though Terry claimed it was in reality a rusty nail that went right through his boot when he was playing football.

When Terry left the army a year after Dave, he went

and looked him up. Dave was just setting up the fruit business at the time and asked Terry to join him. 'The rest is history.'

We packed up around five and set off to go and pick up the rest of the team – they all had a similar story to tell and seemed very happy with their results. They hadn't taken as much cash as we had, but they weren't here for their sales skills, were they? We dropped them off at the hotel and went to meet Dave down the road. He wanted an update in person on how it had gone but couldn't quite be arsed to drive the whole way.

We met him in a lay-by (of course), about twenty miles away from the New Forest. He looked as suspicious as a Dave could look; in a black outfit, smoking a fag with a beanie on, pacing around near his car. Men over fifty probably shouldn't wear beanies; maybe it was a balaclava. Would that be better or worse? We chatted briefly about the day's business, and Terry told him it was all in hand, and that we'd be ready when they returned.

Dave had other ideas.

"The best form of defence is attack," he said, putting out his fag end with a heavy black boot. He strolled over to his car boot and opened it. "So we aren't going to wait for them to come back, we're going to take the fight to them."

He pulled out a couple of cans of petrol and handed them over.

"I've found out where these fuckers keep their fruit. You two are going to go and disrupt their supply chain." He passed Terry a piece of paper with an address on it.

"It's like the Battle of the Bulge — cut off their fuel, and we win the war."

Me and Terry cast a confused glance at each other as the reference flew over our heads.

He sensed our confusion. "Sorry, I've been watching the History Channel again."

Terry laughed.

"That's it, fuck off, and Terry, you can double fuck off. I've seen you watching *World War II in Colour*, you cunt."

He spun around and, with an over-the-shoulder Dave-wave, walked off and got in his car. I wondered why he'd dressed up.

We loaded the petrol cans into the back of Terry's Range Rover and jumped in the front. He typed the address from the piece of paper into his sat-nav. Thirty-four minutes, it chirped.

Thirty-three minutes later, we arrived; Terry was a man who lived to beat his sat-nav. He had a strange relationship with it; he loved its help but felt like he could do better by himself (he couldn't).

We pulled into a small lane with wooden office buildings and ancient-looking warehouses. The place looked like a rural French business park from the 18th century. It had a totally different vibe from our one at home — much less metal. It was lined with trees and hedges, and the buildings were all single-story wooden-panelled affairs.

We pulled over when the sat-nav told us too.

"Any idea which one?"

Terry looked at the piece of paper Dave had given him

and looked up and down the street. "It's number 8."

I couldn't see any numbers on anything.

"It says 'Fat Cow' next to it," he added helpfully.

I looked over the road trying to make out the building numbers. There was a burger van in front of the building just over the road. I suddenly saw what it was called.

'Fat Cow Burgers'.

"There it is," I said. "Look - 'Fat Cow Burgers'."

"What a prick," he said scrunching up the piece of paper and jumping out.

I got out and walked over to the front of the warehouse, this was the one, there was a big number 8 on the door that had been hidden from view. It was a large, sprawling old wooden building with a slate roof and big barn doors at the front.

The place seemed pretty quiet. I went back to Terry, who was fucking around with his night-vision goggles, which were playing up, so I went to take a quick peek inside the warehouse. I wanted to check it was empty – I didn't need a murder charge on top of the ever-increasing list of crimes we'd clocked up this week. I was already having ever-growing doubts about whether this was my best route to normality and a fulfilled life as a proper adult member of society. Yet here I was with a lunatic of some flavour, getting ready to burn down a warehouse to help a man who quit the army after a footballing accident to sell more fruit. Fuck my life!

I popped down a side alley. There was old junk and bins full of rotten fruit everywhere – sure signs we were in the right place. I disturbed a couple of foxes eating from a bin – who knew foxes loved old strawberries? The whole place stunk even worse than ours, it smelt like the fruit had fermented into a new brand of hipster strawberry booze. I pushed one of the bins over to a window and climbed up on top of it to get a proper look in. The place seemed deserted – all the lights were off, and there was no sign of life. I could see punnets and fruit boxes in the moonlight scattered around the main room. I jumped down and pushed the bin back to where it had come from, and made my way back to the car.

Terry had given up on his night-vision goggles and was at his open boot. He'd probably bought them from one of those awful gadget shops you can find in every shopping centre these days. They didn't look like proper army ones – he was too tight to fork out for those, I guessed.

We both grabbed a can of petrol and headed over to the warehouse. I hadn't done this before, so I followed Terry's lead. He seemed to know what he was up to. We poured petrol over the entrance to the warehouse and around the side where all the rubbish and junk was. Terry poured the last of the petrol into a glass bottle he had produced from nowhere and, after soaking a rag and stuffing it in, passed it to me.

"You've done one of these before?"

"No, first time," I said.

"Well fucking light it, chuck it and let's get out of here."

I lit the rag and threw the bottle at the pile of petrol-soaked rubbish that was stacked against the side of the warehouse. The glass shattered, and the petrol lit as it splashed outwards, covering the rubbish in a burning layer of red and yellow flames. The rest of the petrol caught light, and the pile burst into flames. Unfortunately, so did one of my sleeves, as the wind blew the flames towards me. I must have spilt a bit when I was sploshing it everywhere. I started hitting my burning arm frantically, trying to put myself out, like someone on a bad trip attempting to kill all the tiny imaginary spiders crawling down their arm.

"I'm a bit on fire," I said as calmly as I could manage.

Terry took his jacket off and quickly wrapped it around my arm, putting me out.

"Thanks."

"Try not to pour it on yourself next time," he laughed.

We turned and legged it to the car.

Ten seconds later, we were out of the estate and back on the road. My hands were shaking, and I could smell the horrible smell of my singed arm hair. It smelt like a turkey farm I'd been taken to as a kid, which had put me off turkey for life.

I could already see a massive plume of black smoke pouring off the estate as we left. We headed back to the hotel and made our way as quietly as possible to our rooms. I jumped in the shower straight away and put all my clothes in one of the hotel's laundry bags, which I left outside my door.

Smelling a bit less like an arsonist, I decided to call it a day and collapsed on the hotel bed, quickly passing out.

# CHAPTER 11
# WILD HORSES

I was woken at about seven by endless banging on my door. I dragged myself up, half-expecting it to be the police. "Who is it?" I asked through the door. Thankfully, it was only Terry.

"Come on, get your arse up," he shouted through the closed door.

I opened it and blinked at him as the sunlight poured into my room from the bright corridor. He looked far too well-rested for the amount of sleep he must have had. I had more of a student training regime, so to me, it seemed like an ungodly time to be so fucking noisy.

"Fucking chirpy, aren't you? Give me five minutes to stick some clothes on," I mumbled to him.

"I'll meet you down at the restaurant," he said.

A few minutes later, I emerged and made my way down through the confusing warren of corridors to the restaurant. Somehow I managed to walk past the reception twice – the person at the desk spotted it, and I could see them smirking to themselves. It was one of those weird hotels that seemed to have an almost endless set of routes to the lobby. I started thinking I was going the right way, and then, five minutes later, I was lost and confused. All the corridors looked the same, with red patterned carpets and framed photos of cows and fields. It had a distinct aroma of industrial cleaner and burnt toast.

Just when I was about to give up, sit on the floor and have a little cry, I popped out randomly into the restaurant through a side door. I tried to style it out as if I'd meant to come that way. Terry and his squad of army friends were all eating at the table. Luckily, they hadn't noticed my confused entrance. I went and joined them and poured myself a coffee. They were all chipper and super army-ish, but I guess the one thing (other than all the killing and weapons) that the army taught you was how to get up super fucking early and get on with stuff. I gulped back a couple of coffees, and slowly life started to come back into focus.

I realised they were talking about some crazy shit that happened on their last tour together in Afghanistan.

"Remember when we found all that scag?" said one of them, as you do over your morning eggs.

They all laughed.

"Yeah, that was a lot of brown, wasn't it?"

They all nodded and agreed – it was, it seemed, a very large pile of heroin; they continued to eat while nodding at the memory of its enormity.

"What did you do with it?" I foolishly asked.

"We fucking sold it," said the biggest of them, a great big Northern bruiser with anchor tattoos and forearms the size of my legs. He was, of course, called Little Kev, and he had a proclivity for pink cravats, one of which he was sporting now. It was very distracting.

"Sold it to some guy in the air force," said Terry

"Fucking flyboys," Little Kev muttered with a mouth full of sausage.

I decided to go and get some breakfast from the buffet. It was the usual turgid collection of fried British filth. The bacon looked like strips of ham, and the scrambled eggs had a pool of water collecting in the bottom of the tray. I tentatively put the least disgusting-looking piece of bacon and a spoonful of scrambled eggs on my plate, along with a piece of very dry toast, and headed back to the table. I drank a lot more coffee and poked around at the eggs. I just about managed half a piece of bacon. At least the coffee was good.

We finished up and headed to the minibus to drop everyone off at their spots. Gregg was sat on the bonnet smoking a fag waiting for us; he'd come down for the day to help with reloads.

"Adam, good to see you my friend; Dave send me to help you. I bring van full of fruit," he said, offering me a cigarette which I gladly took.

"OK, cool; who's looking after refills at home?"

"We try out, my brother. Dave finally gave him a chance. I ask him for years. He always say he looks too much like a foreigner, he not trust him."

"Jesus, that's a bit strong."

"A bit strong? What do you mean?"

"You know. A bit much." That didn't help. The English language is confusing. "It's a bit of a horrible thing to say," I said.

"Yes. OK. Bit strong. I remember that. Yes, is not very nice thing to say. But Dave is always nice to me, so I think is OK."

How was everyone OK with this shit, I thought. I'd have told him to fuck off. He looks a bit fucking foreign, seriously? Perhaps there was another reason that Dave didn't want to say. I can't imagine what could be more insulting than calling someone too foreign for a job. But you never know.

"Let's hope he's up to the job and doesn't piss Dave off."

"Yes, I hope too," he said nervously.

I put out my cigarette and got in the van with him. "Just follow the minibus and get the hang of the route," I told him. I'd had enough early morning army banter and could do with some quiet morning time. He popped a CD into the old stereo, and "You're Beautiful" by James Blunt came on far too loudly – was there a good volume for Blunt in the morning?

We drove behind the minibus with a seemingly endless stream of Blunt hits pouring out. I had a shifty through some of the other CDs; they were almost all Tina Turner. I stuck with Blunt as the lesser of two evils. We dropped off the first few teams and grabbed some fruit and cream from the back for them. Everyone was dropped off and stocked up with fruit within thirty minutes, and we made our way to the same lay-by from the day before. Gregg had decided to base himself at the end of our lay-by with all the extra fruit. It was already getting hot, and I think the big tree at the end was his best chance for a bit of shade to stop the fruit from completely melting and stinking out his van.

I set up the stall while Terry had a catch-up with him. The first customers arrived within seconds – a nice old couple on their way to see their son in Portsmouth for the day. They seemed delightfully cheerful and asked if I was local. I lied and pretended I was, naming somewhere we'd driven through the day before as my new adopted home. Of course, they knew it well.

"You know Malcolm down the pub then?" they asked enthusiastically, sensing a possible connection with me.

"Yes," I lied, "doesn't everyone? I was down there yesterday."

"It's been shut for weeks now, hasn't it? For a refurb?"

"It was open when I was there," I said, digging myself deeper.

"How odd," they both said together, looking at each other as if I had a screw loose.

I got them their change and hoped no more questions would be forthcoming.

"Did you hear about that fire down the road last night?" they asked.

I tried not to look too interested. "No, where was that then?"

"Down the old Appleyard estate. A couple of warehouses burned down; you could see the flames all the way down by the coast."

"I hope nobody was hurt?"

"No, apparently not – probably those Travellers that were down on the level last week."

"Bloody pikey wankers," his wife unexpectedly spat out with genuine bile.

"I don't think we call them pikeys anymore," I said to her, thinking maybe she just needed re-educating. She was pretty old, and maybe back in her day, whenever the fuck that was, that kind of language was OK.

"Back in my day…" she answered me. I sighed with exhaustion at the thought of where this sentence was going. "Our local pub had a 'No Gypsies' sign."

"Well hopefully it's been replaced with a 'No Racist Cunts' one now," I suggested helpfully.

They turned around and stormed off towards their car. I was relieved that the previous night had only been a bit of arson. I quite enjoyed it, if truth be told. There was something about starting fires that gave me a weird little buzz. Am I an arsonist, I thought? Surely not – maybe at worst, a twisted firestarter.

I served the next couple of people and noticed Terry walking back towards me up the lay-by; he was walking quickly and kept glancing over his shoulder. I went to grab my bat. Were we about to be attacked?

He wasn't alone…

He seemed to have made some friends and had about ten ponies sauntering along behind him. He looked slightly concerned, and every few feet would turn around to give them a polite shoo away; it was having no effect and, if anything, seemed to be encouraging them. The New Forest was a weird place; ponies and donkeys roamed around completely freely. They were constantly on the road, causing some hilariously quaint traffic jams. I didn't know Terry had made their acquaintance.

"New friends?" I asked.

"They're fucking following me," he said, hiding behind the stall from them.

I offered one a strawberry; it didn't seem that interested. Sadly I didn't have a carrot – I suspect they wouldn't have sold very well.

"They seem nice," I said, rubbing him on the side of the head (the horse, not Terry).

Terry retreated towards the minibus. "I'll just be in here for a bit."

"OK," I laughed.

The ponies didn't seem too interested in me, but Terry had got them going. Maybe it was his aftershave or just that perverse animal instinct to always be the most intrigued with the person who shows them the least interest. They soon had him surrounded as about five of them encircled the minibus, and one tried to get him to open the window.

I left them to it and went back to serving customers. Tourists loved the ponies, and they quickly pulled an extra-big queue in. Strawberries and horse-stroking – they were like the traffic jams of our area, but with bigger tails and fewer traffic cones. I had a queue about ten people deep after about five minutes, and the normally fairly shy ponies seemed like they weren't going anywhere. Terry was stuck in the van, looking increasingly unhappy with the situation. Perhaps I should remind him of his comments to Gregg when he hid from the Labradors; perhaps not, though. Maybe he'd start to like them when he realised they were making us extra money. One of the male ones seemed to have taken an extra shine to him and was nudging the window and making some slightly strange noises. I'd have been pointing and laughing if I hadn't been so busy.

After about an hour, or probably what seemed like several to Terry, the ponies got bored at the lack of Terry and sauntered off down the road to see what other chaos they could get into. The moment they left, my queue died down, and after the coast was clear, a slightly flustered Terry emerged.

"Have they gone?"

"Yes, I think you're safe now."

"I fucking hate horses," he snarled.

"They're ponies, Terry," I corrected him.

"Fuck off," he replied curtly.

"Well, they certainly seemed to like you; I think that big one wanted you as his mate."

"Fuck off."

I told him about the report from the old couple about the fire. He was very happy with the news, and all thoughts of randy ponies soon receded. He called Dave to give him an update while I served a funny and very red couple from the Midlands who couldn't stop telling me about their fucking caravan.

The rest of the day passed uneventfully. A few more ponies passed through, and some donkeys caused a traffic jam. Gregg drove back and forth, dropping off fruit; occasionally, the sound of James Blunt or Tina Turner would fill the air as he sped past. I think the army boys were finally getting into the swing of selling. No trouble at any of the lay-bys at all – everything was going smoothly. Hopefully, they were still reeling from our warehouse attack. But I had no doubt they'd be back.

Dave was still in war mode. He said we needed to cement our position rapidly by hiring some locals to run the stalls. We only had the army for another few days; after that, we were on our own with, I'd imagine, a bunch of caravan-dwelling pensioners Dave had recruited from the local bingo.

That evening we left the army in the bar at the hotel and headed off for some staff recruiting. We badly needed some outsiders as all the locals knew each other and were third cousins twice removed. So we set off for the Solent University campus to meet an old friend called Doris from my days at uni. I can't even remember if that was his real name, though it seemed doubtful – who the fuck would name their son Doris? I hadn't ever met his parents, though, so you never know. I'd called him the night before to get things sorted and find some cash hungry students.

Doris was a small-time dealer at my university; he lived in halls opposite me, so we'd met quite early on. I'd even partnered up with him for a while to sell a bit of hash in my last year, when the student loan wasn't cutting it anymore. He seemed to have embraced the campus-dealing lifestyle. He hadn't done quite so well with the whole educational thing and had taken four and a half years to get a third in Business Studies. Since then, he'd been enrolling in different universities every few years and becoming everybody's favourite drug dealer. Now in his mid-thirties, he was starting to blend in a little less on campus than he used to.

We pulled down a little lane and into one of the campus car parks; Doris was there waiting for us and signalled us into a parking space. He looked exactly the same as when I had last seen him a few years before. His long hair was down past his shoulders; he was wearing black jeans and a white tee, and he was covered in tattoos down both arms and creeping up his neck. They seemed to have got closer to his face since I last saw him.

I jumped out, gave him a big hug, and introduced him to Terry.

"Adam says you're the man on campus then," said Terry. "Did you manage to get us some new people?"

"Yes indeed, yes indeed." He sparked up a spliff and took a big drag. "Follow me, Terry."

We walked around the outside of a student accommodation building as we chatted shit about drugs.

"Smashing it down here, mate, if you ever fancy a career change?"

"I'm good, thanks, mate," I said, taking his offered spliff and having a few drags before passing it back.

"I'm trying to have a fresh start without anything dodgy."

Terry chuckled.

"And how's the course going?"

"Yeah, great, all of my course are a right bunch of ketheads, easiest money I've ever made. Half the time, they forget they just paid me," he laughed.

"It wasn't quite what I meant."

He stubbed the spliff out on the wall to a building, waved a key fob at the security system, and in we went. We jogged up a flight of stairs after him and made our way into an open flat. Inside, the air was thick with weed smoke, and about fifteen students were all either skinning up or smoking in the living room. The walls were covered in cult film posters and hip-hop album covers. There was a record player in the corner and vinyl all over the floor.

"Fucking students," Terry muttered under his breath.

Doris turned the music down and flicked the light switch on and off a few times to get their attention.

"Right then, these are the friends of mine I told you about. They are paying a tenner an hour plus bonuses. Cash! All you've got to do is stand around in the sun and sell people strawberries and cream. That's about the gist of it, isn't it?" he said to me.

Terry decided to take control of the proceedings.

"Yes, that's about it. We start at eight am, so if you're going to struggle with that, you might as well fuck off now."

Everyone looked around at each other to see if anyone would leave; they didn't. Possibly just because they couldn't be arsed to stand up.

Terry talked them through the bonuses and what they would have to do. Doris would meet them in the car park every morning as we'd arranged. He was getting a nice kickback from each wage, and we'd agreed that anyone with outstanding debt on his rather large tick list would be paid straight to him until they were square. We didn't fill the students in on that detail as I'm not sure it would have motivated them. That's the trouble with uni dealing, Doris would always complain – tick lists as long as an application form for a student crisis loan.

I could see Terry losing the room slightly; they had all started chatting again. He was like the dad at a bring-your-parent-to-school day. I gave Doris a little nudge to wrap things up.

"OK fuckwits, eight tomorrow morning. Any questions? No, good!"

We made our way back through the flat to the door. Doris said he would stay as he had to sort some bits out. Terry thanked him, and we made our way back to the car. He seemed a little worried they might not be up to scratch, but I assured him that at least a few would be. The usual semi-retired French holidaying caravanners weren't going to cut it around here anyway – not this year, at least. We needed some non-locals who wouldn't run to the police if anything kicked off, and could at least partially take care of themselves. This lot seemed to just about fit the bill. One handy thing about drug-taking students – they rarely called the police.

"We'll see, won't we?" Terry said as he got into the car and headed back to the hotel.

At eight o'clock the next morning, we had about twelve fairly fresh-looking students and a bleary-eyed Doris. He passed me a much-needed coffee and a much less-needed spliff.

I took a quick drag and passed it back. "Bit early for me these days."

The coffee I kept.

We loaded the students up onto the minibus. The army guys were already setting up the stalls (they'd have happily started at 5am if we wanted them), and we dropped a pair of students at each location for the first of a couple of days of training. The army were going to keep an eye out for any trouble and do a bit of fruit prep. They, of course, had brought their own very large knives for the fruit-cutting task.

We said goodbye to Doris; he wasn't coming with us and was off back to bed for most of the day. He was in danger of becoming vampiric.

We pulled into the last lay-by to set up. We had two students with us, so it would hopefully be an easy, relaxing day watching them do all the work. The sun was out in full force, and after showing them what to do, I walked into the field for a quick lie down on the mossy grass; the drag of a spliff I'd had with Doris had hit me quite hard. This was so much more peaceful than the lay-bys where we normally worked. I could hear a little stream tricking along, the occasional laughter from the two students, and a background hum of traffic chugging along the road. I could feel my eyes slowly closing.

I woke up with a start, a massive pony's head nudging me awake. It was Terry's friend from the other day – I recognised it from the funny quiff of blond hair it had. Funny-looking chap. He looked a bit like Donald Trump.

I walked back over to the lay-by to find a queue of

tourists with the two students and Terry serving them as fast as they could. I went to help out.

"Where the fuck have you been?" Terry growled at me under his breath.

"Sorry, I was just having a little nap, your friend woke me up."

"My friend?"

I pointed over to the pony that was heading our way.

"Fuck's sake," said Terry retreating to the minibus again.

Ponies soon surrounded him. Donald had brought his friends; perhaps he wanted to show them Terry.

After we'd got rid of the queue of tourists, I went to help him out. I'd stolen a few carrots from the restaurant the day before and offered one to Terry's handsome friend; he was keener for it than he had been for the strawberry and nibbled the carrot out of my hand.

"Come on, mate, he's harmless; come out here and stop fucking around."

Terry didn't look happy with my comments, but not wanting to lose face with the students, he sheepishly opened the door and took a carrot from me. He offered it to his friend, who snaffled it down in no time. Terry nervously patted him on the head. It seemed like their friendship was finally blossoming.

With ponies, come queues, and by the time Terry had finished his bonding sessions with Donald, there was a lay-by full of cars and a long line of people stroking ponies and buying strawberries and cream. If only we could persuade the ponies to stay in the lay-by each day, we'd be onto a traffic jam winner once again. I guess giving everyone a bag of carrots might be a good start. I'd have to check if carrots were good for them or if it was a myth invented by carrot marketing teams.

My phone rang – it was Dave. I passed a cone of strawberries to Terry to finish off and told him I'd be back in a second. I walked halfway down the lay-by, sparked up a fag, and answered, hoping he didn't want anything too horrific. He'd been having a bit of trouble back on our home turf. Apparently, a few people had been no-shows for shifts, and Gregg's brother had turned out to be a completely fucking useless twat. Dave's words, not mine. I told him about Terry's new friend; he wasn't overly interested or impressed.

"Well, glad you're having such a wonderful time – it's fucking chaos up here. Get your arse back here and you can start running the whole area. Gregg's brother is fucking useless, and Terry can stay there to keep an eye on things and hang out with his new friends."

I hung up and went to say goodbye to Terry and the students. Gregg gave me a lift back to the hotel, and I jumped in my car and headed back home to meet Dave.

# CHAPTER 12

# THAT ESCALATED QUICKLY

It took me the best part of an hour to get back, and as I pulled into the warehouse, Dave was just sending whom I presumed to be Gregg's brother packing with his usual grace and dignity. A couple of strawberries hit my car windscreen as I parked. Dave's management technique seemed largely based on throwing as much fruit at someone as possible until they understood just how angry he was with them. Gregg's terrified-looking brother scurried past me and made off down the street.

"Don't fucking come back, you useless cunt," came booming out of the warehouse, with what I hoped was a final handful of cherries. Dave saw me at the side of the doors.

"Glad you're back, Adam; get your arse in here and let's get things up to speed. Fucking useless twat, he was."

It turned out Harold (Gregg's brother) did not quite have the same work ethic as his brother – in fact, he'd been late with all the fruit deliveries. God knows what he'd been up to. It wasn't exactly complicated. The final straw had come for Dave when one of his staff had given Harold some cash earlier that day, and he'd 'forgotten' to give it to Dave. Dave was predictably fuming and must have called him a "thieving foreign cunt" about fifteen times in the conversation.

"Anyway, sort it out. I've got a meeting to go to. Lock up when you're done, and I'll see you tomorrow."

He chucked me a set of warehouse keys and jumped into his car. Well, it was at least good to be back on home turf. I wasn't looking forward to the next round with the commoners. I said hello to the fruit unpackers, who all looked happy to see the back of Dave, and went up to the office. Hans was in there counting cash – he had a pretty large pile and a couple of familiar-looking bags at his feet. He nodded at me and then looked angrily down at the paper as if I'd made him lose count.

I flicked through the clipboard on the desk to see who was working in which lay-by, gave a confused-looking Hans a wave and went and loaded up the fruit. I told the fruit unpackers I'd be back in an hour and not to slack off because Dave was on his way back. He wasn't coming back today, but they didn't need to know that. Just the possibility of a red-faced fruit flinging Dave was enough to get them working at double speed. I wasn't entirely sure about some of their legal statuses, so maybe that's why they put up with his shit. The abuse and fruit he hurled at them was mind-numbing. I was thankful I wasn't on the receiving end of it.

Twenty minutes later, I unloaded a couple of boxes at the first lay-by with one of our regular sellers. He had his underling with him, who was selling directly to the cars in the traffic jam. It was amazing that nobody had questioned our fake traffic jams so far.

"Alright, mate," I said as I plonked down a load of strawberries.

"So glad you're back. That other lad was a right doughnut; he kept coming up with cherries when I wanted strawberries; he forgot the cream about a dozen times. I don't know where you found him."

"Yeah, sorry about that, but I'm back now."

I spent a few minutes chatting about his motorhome and how the motor was shot. My suggestion that he should have bought a caravan didn't seem to go down too well, and I was off again to the next drop-off.

James was next on my list; it only took me a minute to get to his spot. As soon as I pulled into the lay-by, I could tell something wasn't right. There were three motorbikes between me and the stall, with a very nervous-looking biker sitting on one of them, glancing over his shoulder every few seconds. His bike was still on. The other two were down the far end with their backs to me and helmets still on at the fruit stall. I don't think the student helping him sell had noticed anything weird going on; he was talking to a family at the traffic jam. It looked like they were robbing the stall to me. Lookout, helmets on, cash business. Fuck. One of the bikers at the stall pushed James onto the floor, confirming my thoughts. The other one kicked him while he was down. Double fuck!

I called Hans and told him to get his arse down here. I revved up my car's pathetic engine as much as possible and accelerated towards the three bikes. I made it up to about twenty mph before I hit them. The first bike flew into the road. The lookout saw me coming at the last minute. He just managed to jump off his bike as I made contact. I'd trashed all three bikes but missed him completely. Smoke poured out of my poor car – I think I'd killed it.

I jumped out of the smoking car, bat in hand. The lookout was lying half in the hedge. I smashed him hard around his helmet. I was getting the hang of this. He slumped back on the floor, completely sparked out. I looked up at the other two, who had left the fruit stall and were running back towards their bikes. One had something shiny in his hand – not a gun, but a fucking large knife.

In for a penny, I thought and sprinted towards them. I took a massive swing at the first one. He had his visor up, and I made eye contact as the bat smashed into his helmet. I could almost feel the vibrations – he looked like Wile E. Coyote after another Acme explosion gone wrong. It was game over, and he collapsed on the floor, holding his head.

The third one was more of a problem – he slashed at me with the knife, I managed to get an arm up to protect myself, I felt the blade tear through my shirt and flesh. I couldn't feel any pain with all the adrenaline flying around my body.

I was in slow-motion mode. I could almost feel myself coming out of my body and seeing the whole thing from above. I pulled myself back together with a head shake and took a swing at his hand, making contact with the knife and a few knuckles. It flew into the hedge. He backed off a few feet, suddenly not quite so confident. His friend was coming round and started getting back up, and they both started edging towards me. I stepped back a few feet. They stepped forward a few feet. They were like circling hyenas, and I was the wildebeest. I took a few mild swings at them to keep them back. They separated and started to move around me on both sides. Fuck, I'd seen this David Attenborough documentary.

It never ended well for the wildebeest.

Suddenly there was an almighty bang that sounded like nothing on earth – a mix of bones and metal – as a white van smashed into one of them. His body flew through the air, crashing down about twenty metres up the lay-by, crumpled and lifeless. It was Hans; he'd come to the rescue. I turned to his friend, who threw himself into the hedge, trying to scramble away from the madness. He hadn't anticipated how overgrown these British summer hedges get and only made it halfway in. His legs dangled out of the back as he tried to scramble away through the brambles and branches. I grabbed a boot and pulled.

"James, give me a fucking hand."

We pulled him backwards out of the hedge together.

I looked around to see Hans out of the white van, taking care of the already stunned and injured lookout. His helmet was off, and he was being punched endlessly in the face by Hans. I told the little shit whose leg I had to take his fucking helmet off. He obliged and begged me not to hurt him as he watched Hans dealing with his friend. I got James to grab some cable ties we used to keep the stalls together. We cable-tied his hands behind his back and turned him face-down onto the floor. I stood with a foot on his head, like a big game hunter with his sad trophy, watching Hans at work. He was very efficient and fairly terrifying. Once he'd finished punching the lookout unconscious. He turned his attention to the motionless body of the man he'd hit on arrival. After walking fairly casually over to his body, he got hold of a leg and dragged him to the back of the van, leaving a red trail. He checked his pulse and then tossed him in like a sack of potatoes.

While he was shutting the door, the seemingly unconscious lookout, lept in the air as if jolted with a million volts.

I was so stunned all I could get out was "er Hans..." as I pointed towards the problem.

The dazed lookout took a few steps towards the road while looking over at us. A huge lorry swept passed and clipped him around the head with its mirror. The snapping noise as his head spun round and his neck snapped was as loud as a gunshot.

Hans legged it over to his crumbled corpse and called James over to help him, they hauled his body to the back of the van and threw him in. Then Hans headed over to me with a wild look in his eyes.

"Fucking pricks," he said, taking a massive swinging kick into the side of the one I had on the ground. "Get his leg," he shouted at me.

We grabbed a leg each and dragged him across the tarmac to the back of the van. He was still conscious and looked terrified. We lifted him up on his feet and pushed him backwards into the pile of his friends' bodies in the back of the van.

"Keep fucking eye on them," he ordered me.

He made his way back to the motorbikes and stood each one up and pushed them into the hedge. He came back to the van and grabbed a couple of big bottles of liquid from the front seat. He splashed it over the blood stains and threw the bottles into the hedge where the bikes were.

He jumped into the back of the van and told me to go and get James and the kid back to work. I walked over to James, trying to look like this was all normal.

"Looks like I arrived just in time, mate," I said.

"Yeah, horrible cunt pulled a knife on me and then punched me in the face. I'm sixty-seven; what's wrong with people?" He seemed unsurprisingly shaken by the whole thing. I don't think he'd even realised two of them were probably dead.

"Well, sorry about that, we'll deal with them. Can you and your helper get back to work and pretend nothing happened? Finish up in an hour or so, and we'll call you later."

"I guess so."

"Thanks, see you later." I spun around and made my way to the van. Hans was already in the driver's seat, and there was a pile of assorted bodies in the back.

A worried-looking student was lurking at the back of the van. I gave him a cigarette and told him there'd be a £50 bonus if he kept quiet about this.

He seemed pretty happy with that, so I sent him over

to James to get back to work.

"What now?" I asked Hans.

"Dave wants to speak to them."

"Are any of them able to talk still?"

"One of them. Other two are dead, I think."

"Fuck," I thought and said. Perhaps now was a good time to call the police. But perhaps not.

"You are hurt?" He asked.

"Shit, yes." I'd nearly forgotten. I took my jacket off and rolled my sleeve up. My arm was covered in blood and there was a 3 or 4-inch gash down the side of my arm.

"Is no problem, I patch up now." Said Hans, pulling a first aid kit out from behind his seat.

"I train in the army, don't worry is just a little scratch."

He washed my arm down with water, sprayed something on it, stuck some sticky little stitch things over the wound, popped a dressing on and was done in no time.

"Well shit, thanks Hans, you weren't kidding."

"No, I am not a kidder. Keep it wrapped for few days, don't get wet and make sure doesn't get infected."

He started up the van, pulled out of the lay-by, and we drove off down the road away from the crime scene, which never was. We went for a few miles into the middle of nowhere, turned off the main road down a farm track and bumped our way down it for a mile or two before turning into a farm entrance. We came to a halt in front of an old run-down pair of barns. A couple of chickens ran out of one of them and into a field. Dave appeared out of the same barn, wearing a white all-in-one hazmat suit outfit, complete with gloves and boots. He had a couple of large black sacks in his hand.

"Good work, lad," he said, patting me on the shoulder. He was the proud psychotic father I never wanted.

We opened up the van and dragged the first still-breathing body out onto the mud and chicken shit.

"He's the only one that made it," said Hans.

Dave and Hans grabbed him by an arm each and dragged him into the barn, emerging a minute later without him.

"Right, let's get these two sorted," Dave said.

He unrolled one of the black sacks, and I helped Hans pull one of the bodies out of the van onto the sack. He wrapped it around him and zipped it up. He had a massive roll of thick black gaffer tape with him, and he started wrapping it tightly around the bag until he'd made a shiny black cocoon.

"Next," Dave said to Hans.

We repeated the process until we had two gigantic butterfly cocoons wrapped up on the floor. This was madness; we were disposing of bodies now. Perhaps my thoughts on this job not being like the mafia were a little naïve. I'm so far out of my depth here.

Hans and I picked up the first one and followed Dave around the side of one of the barns. Round the back, there was a large field with about twenty square metres cut out of it, ready for some building foundations. There was a massive hole in the centre and a cement mixer already spinning nearby. We tossed the first cocoon into the middle of the hole and went back to get the next one. We arrived back a few minutes later and dumped the second one in next to him. Dave moved the cement mixer around and started pouring. Once they were covered and the machine was empty, he jumped out of the hole and made his way to a door at the side of the barn.

He slid the big wooden door open – chickens flapped around on top of old farm equipment, and a pig ran around the back of the barn and out of the door. We walked to the middle of the barn, where a large metal chain was slung over one of the wooden beams. Attached to it was a semi-conscious bleeding man. The floor was covered with animal shit and straw; the place smelled like the country. A collection of worrying-looking tools were laid on a table next to the lightly swinging man. There was a power drill, a saw, a small blowtorch (the kind you might make a crème brûlée with), a couple of hammers and, very noticeably, a bottle of Matey bubble bath.

"You can leave now," Dave said to me. "Hans and I will take care of this. Can you take the van and go and set fire to it somewhere you can walk home from?"

"OK, no problem. What about the bikes?"

"I've got a friend collecting them, so don't worry, just go home and relax and come in tomorrow as if nothing happened."

Relax, I thought. Was he fucking joking?

"I've got to ask. I'm sure I'll regret it. What's with the bubble bath?"

Hans laughed and picked up the bottle of Matey. He forced the man's mouth open and poured some in. He started choking. Hans held his hand over his mouth.

Bubbles were coming out of the side.

"OK, OK, I get it."

Hans took his hand away, and a jet of bubbles flew out of the man's mouth as he started coughing and spluttering.

"Thanks for the demonstration, I'll see you both tomorrow." I knew I'd regret asking. There goes another happy childhood memory. I used to love that stuff.

"Yes, see you tomorrow. Good work today, you done fucking well," said Dave, playing with the blowtorch.

Hans threw me the keys. He looked calmer now; the wild look in his eyes had finally abated.

"There's some petrol over there," he said, pointing at a jerrycan in the corner. I went and grabbed it and headed out to the van. It looked pretty fucked – the bumper was hanging off, and the windscreen was cracked at the bottom. I jumped in, started it up, reversed it back, and headed out down the country lane we'd come in on.

I hadn't realised the extent of these people's insanity. Did I want to be anything to do with this? They were about to have some kind of medieval human barbecue. It was a long way from selling people some strawberries, a really long fucking way. But it was better to be on their side than not, I suppose.

Thankfully rush hour was in full flow, so nobody would notice another beat-up builder's van. I drove a few miles towards my house to a spot I had in mind. There was a golf course near me which I could easily walk back home from. I arrived a few minutes later and thought I should make it look like joyriders, so I drove through a hedge onto the course. I sped up and skidded across the grass. I always hated the snobbery of golf courses and thought I'd have a few minutes of fun after a very stressful day. The van slipped and slid across the fairway as I made my way to the end of the third hole. I started doing doughnuts around the flag and then spun off onto the fairway of hole five that ran alongside it. I accelerated towards the bunker, and the van slumped into the sand with a groan that it would never recover from. I jumped out and grabbed the petrol; I opened the tank and stuck a petrol-covered rag inside. I poured the rest of the petrol over the front seats and all over the back of the van. I chucked the can inside and stood back to admire my handy work. It looked like a weird, surreal sculpture sticking its arse up out of the sand. I lit the rag, lit the rest of the box of matches and threw them into the back of the van.

The whole thing went up in flames in seconds. It looked amazing, I'd have loved to take a photo, but that would probably be a terrible idea for many reasons. I'd managed not to set myself on fire this time too. I backed off to the eighth hole, about a hundred yards away, and sat down in a bunker to watch the show. I lit a cigarette and took a heavy drag; fuck me, that was a fucking dramatic day. No wonder Terry always looked so stressed. I lay back and watched the van as it was engulfed in smoke and flames. After finishing my cigarette and carefully taking the end with me to leave no DNA. I made my way across the golf course, which was lit by the eery combination of a burning van and a full moon. I was home in about forty minutes, and I don't think anyone saw me the whole time.

I jumped in the shower and washed the day's madness away before bagging up all my clothes and leaving them by the door to dump in a bin the next morning. I sat on the sofa and rolled myself a very strong spliff. I was totally wired. I tried to watch some shit TV, but a slideshow of images from the day kept flying through my brain. What the fuck had I got myself involved in? I just wanted a bit of normality, not this. I kept seeing the two bodies we buried in the cement over and over again in my head.

I'd acted on pure instinct when I saw what was happening at the lay-by. I'd felt a weird rush of something when it was over. What was it? Not adrenaline. Maybe I enjoyed the whole thing. I think perhaps it was the power. I enjoyed the feeling of power. What was I turning into?

The next day I was up early, had another shower and then suddenly I remembered – shit, my car was fucked; where did it even end up? Well, I guess I could get a taxi, or take my bike if I had to. I looked out of my window to the drive, and to my surprise, an old estate was sitting there. I opened it up, and there were keys in the ignition. I guess this was my car now. I suppose it was something of an upgrade and had more room for fruit, so it would do for now. With that, I headed off to the warehouse.

I arrived just as Hans did; his immaculate old-school 316 BMW was gleaming in the sun. It looked like it had been freshly cleaned, and some obscure German synth-pop was blaring out of the speakers as he pulled to a halt.

He cut the engine and jumped out.

"Hello, good morning."

"Hi mate, how's tricks?"

"Good, very good. All cleaned up, very good."

We walked to the warehouse and pulled the doors open at the front. A few of the fruit unpackers were waiting for us. They'd been early ever since Dave had his last outburst at them. We let them in and got them started on the day's work. We started filling up water bottles with cream and filling up cooler bags with the cream bottles. We loaded up my car with strawberries, cream and extra cones. I noticed we weren't using his car. There was no way he was getting cream on that leather.

"Where's Dave?" I asked.

"He is getting insurance and a new van. Someone stole old one last night."

"Oh no, terrible, all the car thieves around here."

"Yes," he laughed. "It was stuck on the golf course where Dave play golf. He said the third hole was a fucking disaster."

"Fucking kids these days."

"Yes, no respect."

We both laughed. I don't think I'd seen Hans laugh before.

We finished loading the car and told the packers that Dave would be along in a minute and to keep up the good work. They looked terrified, as always. We sped out of the car park towards a day of topping up and checking that nobody was trying to rob us.

We dropped off fruit, picked up cash and made sure

everything was running smoothly. Hans was a man of few words and mostly just lurked behind me with a few boxes of fruit and cream ready for the stall. But he was growing on me, and I think I was slowly breaking him; maybe we'd be friends.

"Hans, do you enjoy this job?" I asked him.

"Yes, I love it."

"Fair enough," I replied.

"Adam, I have to tell you something. Now we know each other better."

"OK, what?"

"My name. It's not Hans," said Hans.

"What the fuck is it then?"

"It's Lukas," replied Hans.

"Why the fuck does everyone call you Hans, then?" I asked.

"When I go for interview with Dave, he call me Hans the German, like in the war."

"Did you not correct him?"

"Yes, about fifty times, then I give in. Now everybody calls me Hans."

"Thanks for sharing, Lukas, and nice to meet you finally."

"Good to meet you too, Adam," he laughed.

We stopped off with James next, who was still a bit shaken from the day before; he didn't make eye contact with Hans but otherwise seemed happy enough. I spent the next five minutes chatting with him about Northern France and his next holiday – anything to stop him from freaking out too much about what had happened. He told me he was going to Brittany to stay with some old friends. They'd gone over there on holiday once and had never come back. They properly loved it, he said and had bought a small house out there. They couldn't speak a word of French when they moved, but somehow managed to get by OK.

"How long have they been there for now?" I asked him, feigning interest.

"About five years."

"They must be nearly fluent by now."

"They can just about ask for a baguette and a glass of wine," he replied.

"Why don't they learn French?" I asked him, now genuinely curious.

"They don't need to, everyone out there is English or speaks English."

"That makes life easier," I replied, giving up.

These caravaners were like a different species. Very occasionally, the poor fuckers' wives hated the whole thing, but in for £50k or more, they got dragged all over Europe and Britain, having a wonderfully terrible time. I'd only met James' wife once, and she seemed like a nice lady, but she looked more like a golf resort on the Costa del Sol might be her thing.

As we finished our fascinating chat, I gave him a few hundred quid as we shook hands and told him it was for yesterday. He seemed happy enough.

As we got back in the car, Hans asked, "Why you talk to these cunts about fucking stupid caravans?"

"Just trying to be polite and make them work well.

Happy employees are hardworking and more trustworthy," I suggested to him.

"Fucking caravans, I hope they explode," he muttered as he turned the stereo back up.

It turns out that nobody likes caravans, not even the Germans.

At about half-three, we got a call from Dave – team meeting back at the warehouse at 4pm. Just when we were having a nice, quiet day, Dave was bound to add some chaos to it. We picked up some cash from one of the last lay-bys and headed back, stopping off for a quick coffee on the way, of course.

We pulled into the warehouse just after four. The fruit unpackers were all making their way out of the warehouse, and happily, there was no fruit flying after them, meaning at least Dave wasn't in an explosive mood. More of a relief for them than us; I quite liked watching him throw fruit at them while they ran around trying to hide from him. It was like watching a bad clown at a kids' party. He was standing at the top of the stairs on the phone, wearing some kind of golfing outfit, a white polo shirt and smart slacks. He looked ridiculous.

He waved us up the stairs, still chatting on the phone before hanging up with his standard 'fuck off'. He spun on his shiny golf shoes and turned into the office; there was a large set of golf clubs on one of the chairs.

"Shut the door and grab a seat," he said. "Coffee?"

He made us both an espresso; Hans moved the enormous golf bag, and we both took a seat.

"Good work yesterday, both of you – we can't let these

cunts try and rob us. Anyway, I had Terry on the phone today – two of his lay-bys got hit by the same pricks, it seems. They got away with about three grand. Little fuckers, predictably just after we'd sent the army lot home."

We both nodded in agreement at how these cunts could indeed not be allowed to get away with it.

"We didn't get anything useful out of that – now buried in cement – cocky little prick we strung up last night. He croaked it before we had a chance to get properly started."

"Too much blowtorch," laughed Hans terrifyingly.

"So, I've had to go and play fucking golf today."

This seemed a little off-topic – maybe it was stress relief for him.

"With an old friend of mine in the police."

"I wondered why you dress like a cunt," said Hans in an unexpected burst of courageous wit.

He ignored the insult. "You know what my police friend said? He said it was those fucking pricks from last year, the fucking Mathews clan, fucking drug dealing pricks."

Dave spat on the ground as if to emphasise his disgust at them, like an Italian peasant woman in an old film.

The fucking Mathews lot again. The same wankers that robbed Mike, or half-robbed Mike at least. Control of the entire South West drug market was evidently not enough for them.

"You know who they are?" Dave asked me.

"Yeah, I've heard of them," I said. "Eight psychotic

brothers and an uncle."

"Well, that isn't fucking strictly true anymore – seven brothers now, as you killed the second-youngest one yesterday when you hit him with the van."

Thankfully, he was looking at Hans when he said this. Hans looked like he couldn't give two fucks, possibly not even one.

"My mate got robbed by them recently too."

"What mate's that, then?" asked Dave.

"Just a friend – he's called Mike, he sells and grows a bit of weed."

"Interesting. Is he OK? What did they take?"

"Yeah, he's OK. If I remember right, about fifteen grand and a few kilos of green."

"Ouch," said Dave, looking pained at the thought.

"They missed his grow room, so he wasn't too bothered."

"I suppose that's something. Thieving little shits."

"He knows where they all live – he just got warned off touching them."

"Does he now? That is certainly some information that would be very fucking helpful. Can you call him and find out?"

"I can try. He's a bit old school and doesn't have a mobile. I'll give his landline a call and leave him a message in a minute. I'll tell you what he says when he gets back to me."

"OK, thanks. So we've got a massive fucking problem – not only do these pricks want to rob us blind, but it seems like, according to my friend, they want to take over our pitches and start selling from them."

"Fruit?" asked Hans.

"Fruit and other shit, I'd imagine. The police, as you can probably imagine, aren't fucking too overwhelmed by this idea. Greedy little pricks. Now that we've killed one, the moment they realise what's happened, they are going to be all over us like a swarm of killer hornets."

"Fuck," I said helpfully.

"Fuck indeed, so we need some help with this as it's bigger than we are, and I'm not getting fucked over for some coke-dealing spots by these cunts."

"So, what's the plan then?" asked Hans.

# CHAPTER 13

# MR BAGUETTE

"We've got some professional help coming in from France. He should be here any minute."

"Not Mr Baguette," said Hans, sounding genuinely worried.

"Yes, Mr Baguette," said Dave.

"Mr Baguette," I laughed nervously. "Who or what is Mr Baguette?"

Hans was staring at the floor.

"Well, at face value, he's a French heavy hitter I know from back in my army days," explained Dave. "He was discharged after taking out three military police with just a baguette. Never touched them with anything else. They were out cold when the reinforcements turned up. He was just sitting there eating his baguette. Since then, he's been called Mr Baguette, and there is always, and I mean always, a baguette involved in his hits. It's his thing, his calling card."

"I always thought he was a baker," said Hans.

"No, he isn't a fucking baker, you daft German cunt. After getting kicked out of the army, he went into private security, which lasted about ten minutes, until there was a nasty incident with a Saudi he was meant to guard. They had a bit of a clash over him smoking on the job. They didn't see eye to eye, and Mr Baguette smashed his teeth out and tried to choke him to death on his lunch."

"A baguette of some kind?" I asked.

"Yes, you're catching on."

"Well, he sounds interesting."

"That's an understatement – he's a lovely chap if you don't piss him off. Since then, he began a new career as a hitman. He concluded, quite rightly, that he was someone that could not deal with members of the public. He loves his work, really loves it. Always very clean, and his reputation in fifteen years has become the stuff of legend. We're very lucky to be able to use him. His client list is quite something in itself these days, I understand."

We headed downstairs while we waited for this curious Frenchman to turn up. I quickly called Mike and left him a message to call me urgently. We needed to get all the cash out of here before any trouble kicked off with the Mathews clan. They were bound to head to our warehouse when they worked out what had happened.

We spent the next forty minutes putting bundles of stinking cash into bags. This cash had a stink unlike any other – it's weird how large amounts of cash has a smell that often gives away its source. Coke money smells of coke, weed money smells a little skunky, and fruit money smells of rotting fruit.

We finished loading up the bags with cash and were just on the last bag when there was a loud bang on the door. I shat myself.

Hans and Dave pulled guns unexpectedly out of their jackets and pointed them at the door.

Why didn't I have a gun? "Where's my gun?" I whispered through the palpable tension in the room.

Dave walked over and opened the door with his gun behind his back.

He stood back as the door swung open. A silhouette of a man in a long raincoat with a cigarette in his mouth and two baguettes under his arm framed the doorway.

Mr Baguette had arrived.

He was a gaunt and very white chap: his short dark hair had grey flecks at the side and his cheekbones protruded worryingly with every drag of his very French-smelling cigarette. He was every part an Englishman's vision of a Frenchman, but he had that thousand-yard stare of a killer. He just needed a chain of onions to complete the look, but I guess he didn't want to look foolish. I could imagine people at a crime scene trying to describe him. They'd seen a Frenchman in a long jacket smoking cigarettes, they'd say. "That's all of them," the detective would reply, much to everyone's xenophobic hilarity. Nobody would suspect such a character could be responsible for the bloodbath down the road.

Dave introduced us to him – always an area of awkwardness for any Englishman. Mr Baguette got stuck in with a couple of kisses for everyone. Hans looked a little taken aback. Dave informed us Mr Baguette would be working here for the next few days and to give him whatever he needed.

"Now fuck off while we have a catch-up and get that

money away somewhere safe. Meet us down at the fancy Italian place in town. We'll be having a bite to eat there."

Dave threw a brick of money at each of us. "That's for the last few days' hard work."

We thanked him, gave Mr Baguette a last handshake and went to stash some bags of cash. It was too late for the banks, so it was off to some of Hans' contacts. There was quite the German community in the local area, much to my surprise – I don't think I'd ever met a German here before, and I had wrongly believed that Hans was just here for the work. We drove fifteen miles or so and pulled up outside a church in a small village in the middle of nowhere.

A German money-laundering vicar, I wondered? A Catholic safe house for Nazi gold? No, that would be too obvious. We both got out of the car and walked around to the small stone church wall. There was a funeral going on inside – I could hear crying and someone reading out a speech, and a large black hearse was parked outside. Hans walked to the driver's window and knocked on it quietly. A red-faced man in a badly fitted suit climbed out, and they shook hands and exchanged some kind of German greeting. They walked to the back of the hearse, and the man opened up the thankfully empty car and slid a panel out in the centre. Hans told me to grab the bags, and we loaded them into a large hole under where the coffin normally sat. With a quick handshake, we were on our way again. That was easy, at least.

We drove into town and met Dave and Mr Baguette in the garden of the small restaurant they were eating in. It was one of the fanciest ones around – you can't give a French hitman substandard English cuisine and expect to get away with it.

We walked through the front doors and told the waiter we were expected, and he pointed us to the outside area. It was all vines, olive trees, white walls and elegant uplighting, with small bistro tables on the cobbled floors. The place reeked of money. Dave waved us over as we appeared. I suspect we looked slightly out of place in the elegant surroundings. We both had fruit splatters all over us, as usual and probably smelt like a Wimbledon bin. We sat with them in the corner of the garden, away from most of the other tables. Dave beckoned us in close.

"I've spoken to Terry, and he's managed to do a deal with the New Forest commoners. Your friend Doris turned out to be worth his weight in gold," said Dave. "He'd been getting his gear off them for years, and Terry went for a sit-down with them. They don't give a fuck about the fruit, it turns out. Although they were a little bit pissed off about the warehouse fire, largely because there was about twenty kilos of skunk stashed under the floorboards."

"Oops," I commented helpfully.

"But we're all friends now – they've been battling the Mathews on the fringes of their borders for years, fighting over the heroin trade mostly, kebab shop takeaway fires, dodgy gear killing junkies and tipped off police raids, the usual sort of thing."

"Bad business," added Hans.

"Yes, fucking quite. Our enemy's enemy is our friend

185

and all that shit," said Dave philosophically. "We've agreed to help them take over the Mathews areas with the aid of our friend here; in return, we get all their lay-bys forever, any backup we need, and a little kickback on their local trade."

Mr Baguette sat and listened, dragging his cigarette and sipping wine. Hans nodded as enthusiastically as he could. I was the only one that still seemed a little worried.

"We've just got to take care of the whole family?" I asked.

"Yeah, that's about it," said Dave, not reacting to my worry or sarcasm.

These people are insane, I thought while pouring some wine into a large glass. This was too much for me. They want to start killing whole families off just to protect their fruit business. I took a large swig. Mr Baguette looked over disapprovingly.

"Slowly, sip it slowly," he said with a strong French accent.

I apologised and took a small sip. "I am a little nervous."

"Don't be. It will be OK, I think."

We all clinked glasses and finished the drinks. Dave chucked a wad of notes on the table, and we headed out.

"You're going to be driving Mr Baguette this evening, Adam," Dave said casually on the way out. "Here you go, take this car." He chucked me the keys to a small new Citroën Cactus. "It's the only car he'll drive in; he's a very loyal Frenchman regarding brands."

"Fuck, Dave, I'm not sure about this," I said honestly.

"Come on, son, we're relying on you. We need someone who knows the area and can blend in. Hans stands out from a fucking mile away. It's got to be you."

"It's too much, Dave. I don't want to be involved in this shit."

"Do you need someone to hold your hand?" said Dave, having had enough of my negative vibes. "This is police-sanctioned, you fucking idiot. You can't get in any shit for it, and you only have to drive him. Stop being a big girl's blouse."

"Fuck's sake," I replied, realising that my objections were pointless. I was doing this. "OK, I guess so."

"Good lad. Now don't worry. I'll look after you," he said, reassuring me much less than I'm sure he meant to.

"OK, bon, we go," Mr Baguette said to me and walked around the side of the Citroën.

I jumped in and adjusted the seat. Dave had been driving it and he was a big fucker. I slid the seat forward and moved the mirror. Mr Baguette was in. I turned the sat-nav on.

"Where to?"

"No sat-nav and turn off your telephone," he said.

I obliged obediently. When he was buckled up, I noticed the two baguettes between his legs.

"Drive to Smiths Towers, you know the place," he said.

Everyone knew the place; if you wanted weed or coke, that was where you went if you didn't have a contact — a right shady shithole.

We pulled up in a dark back-alley ten minutes later, near the tower. Overturned bins and a burned-out car set the scene beautifully; rats scurried around the bins, and the light from a flickering yellow streetlight lent the whole place an ethereal quality.

"You are coming," he said.

"Really, I thought I might wait for you here."

"No, I need to, hmmm, how do you say, look more local."

It was a fair comment – he wasn't blending in around here. I jumped out and grabbed a cap from the back seat. We set off.

"Follow me," he said, the baguettes under his arm, as he trotted out of the end of the alley at a low scuttle. I followed, and we ran across a grass verge to the car park at the back of the towers. He headed straight over to a glass door with a smashed pane which he stuck his hand through and opened from the inside. We slipped into a dank corridor – strip bulbs flickered, revealing broken furniture and piles of rubbish covering everything. The place stank of piss.

We slowly made our way up the corridor, stepping over what looked like human shit and endless needles. There was a smashed door to one side coming up, and I could hear talking; he waved me to take the front. I slowly made my way up to the side of the door. It was just smackheads; I could hear from their tone. They made a whining, weasel-like sound that was always full of lies.

"I'd lend you a tenner if I could. I just gotta wait 'til payday, Debs. Honestly, if I could come and meet you, I'd give you a tenner. I just don't get paid 'til Friday."

I looked around the door; he had his back to us and was sitting on a filthy armchair as he spoke on the phone. A couple of sleeping girls were on an old sofa to one side.

I darted across the opening, stopped and looked back through the door. Nobody had noticed, and I waved my new French friend across. We continued up the corridor; I could see the double doors leading into the main tower entrance lobby. We picked our way through the rubble and needles to the doors. The whole tower must be abandoned now; it used to be half full of druggies and dealers and half-normal people. But I hadn't been here for about a decade and things had changed. It hadn't looked so bad then; I came down once in a while when I was younger and needed some weed or pills. It had certainly turned a corner here. Full-on crack house stylings with hints of heroin and a smidgen of human shit to finish it off.

The concierge was nowhere to be seen.

"OK, now we act like we are buying, yes," Mr Baguette whispered as he stood more upright and walked confidently out into the bright flickering lights of the tower lobby. We walked straight to the second lift and pushed the button. The place had once been a bastion of forward-thinking architecture and social inclusion. I wondered when the last time the architect visited. Did he feel responsible for what it had become, the monster he had helped create?

The lift light lit up on one of the floors near the top and slowly made its way down, occasionally stopping for a second. Just as it got to about the tenth floor, I heard footsteps behind us.

"Be cool," said Mr Baguette.

Both of us just stared at the lift and hoped for the best. The footsteps stopped behind us just as the lift arrived. The doors opened, and the yellow light from the lift poured into the lobby. We walked in, and he pushed the eighteenth-floor button; then we turned to see who was behind us. It was just a junky – thank fuck for that –a young lad with a skinhead and a tattoo of a rat on the side of his head.

"Alright," he said as he walked into the lift and pressed the same button as ours.

We both nodded and muttered greetings to him.

He was buzzing and on an up, so this would be easy. He looked like a scag head who still hadn't fully turned yet; like a secondary character in a zombie movie, he'd been bitten and knew he would change soon, but there was still a flicker of humanity lurking within. His black leather jacket looked like it was worth a few hundred quid. Give him a month, and I'm sure he'd have sold it.

You'd be forgiven for thinking that heroin use was on the decline these days. It's been a long time since *Trainspotting*, and there seemed to be fewer heroin addicts on the streets, didn't there? But looks can be deceiving. Heroin use was alive and well. The junkies were everywhere; they just changed their look. There were still some of your old favourites around, though – hanging out on the street, begging or thieving or both. But a lot of them had died, maybe some had gotten clean, doubtful sadly. The life expectancy of a street junky isn't very high, surprisingly. Now users looked like this guy – more failed rock stars than street junkies. He'd almost pass as a normal person. Almost.

"You here to see Johnny?" he asked.

"Yeah mate, got to get my friend here some coke. He's been clanging since he got here the other day."

"Oh man, I know the feeling; my missus is always banging on about white, blah blah blah, coke coke coke; honestly does me fucking head in."

"Yeah, man, fucking cokeheads."

"More of a brown man myself. I fucking love the stuff."

"Yeah, I can imagine, it's very moreish," I said as the lift doors pinged open on floor eighteen.

We all stepped out into the open-air corridor; our new friend turned left, and we followed. We walked about fifty feet and turned around a corner. Each flat we walked past had smashed windows and no door. A crackhead's Airbnb.

We came to a halt at the first flat on the corridor we turned onto.

The guy knocked twice loudly on the door; we stood just out of sight to his side, he was too high to notice anything was up and too excited about scoring to care.

A metal grid slid open. "Who's that?" someone shouted out of the hole.

"Hi mate, it's me again, can't stay away!"

"It's that prick again," I heard from inside, as a few locks started sliding back.

Mr Baguette pushed me against the wall and whispered for me to stay put. The door cracked open, weed smoke and drum and bass swooshed out into the corridor. Our friend made his way through the door, full of soon-to-be-shattered optimism. Mr Baguette pulled out a gun and screwed on a silencer, tucking his baguettes firmly under an armpit. It always amazed me what a French person could do while carrying baguettes, but this was something else.

The last thing I saw was him kicking the back of the young smackhead's legs so that he fell forward into the room, he walked calmly over him with his gun stretched out in front of him. I heard two dull thuds as he fired, and then the door slammed behind him. I could hear muffled noises through the open flap. A girl screamed, then thuds and the noise of bodies falling. The music went quiet. I waited for what seemed like a lifetime, looking nervously down the corridor, expecting backup to arrive any second. Nobody did. Dogs barked in the background of the estate and motorbikes and mopeds buzzed around the bottom of the tower.

The door flung open after what seemed like a lifetime, and Mr Baguette stood calmly in the frame. He was noticeably missing the baguettes. His gun was snugly tucked away again, but I could still smell the smoky gunpowder from its use. It smelt like fireworks.

"Come," he waved to me. I followed him back in.

It was mayhem inside. There were four bodies in the first room – our junky friend who would never be annoyed by his coke-head missus again, the grunt on the door and two other dealers who were still sitting in the chairs at the table. There were small red dots on their foreheads and blood all over the grimy sitting room wall behind them. I threw up in my mouth as I walked through the carnage. Only my fear of leaving any incriminating DNA stopped me from releasing it, and I swallowed it back down like a good boy. I wasn't cut out for this shit. Mr Baguette looked at me as if to say as much.

I followed him through to the kitchen, relieved to get out of the slaughterhouse. I thought I was meant to just be driving this French murderer around, not helping him with… What was I helping him with? What the fuck were we doing in the kitchen? Why was I here?

"Help me," Mr Baguette said as he walked to the side of a big fridge-freezer at one end of the room. I glanced back through the kitchen to the open bedroom and could see a fat man lying on the floor with what appeared to be about half a baguette sticking out of his mouth. We slid the fridge forward, and there was a hole smashed in the plaster at the bottom. He bent over and vanished inside; I poked my head in after him. It was a small bedroom in the flat next door, and on the bed were two big black bags. I followed him in.

"Take these," he said and zipped up a bag of money. I zipped up the other bag, which was full of weed, coke, brown in baggies, some scales and a few other bits.

"OK, let us go."

He loaded me up with both bags and made his way back through the hole. I squeezed through after him with the bags over my back. I got stuck for a second; he gave me the same look he did when I drank the wine too quickly. I freed myself. We went back to the door and made our way onto the corridor and back to the lift. It was on its way up and had stopped on the second floor; we went straight onto the fire escape stairs. We made our way down the first of eighteen floors as quickly as we could. We were jumping over burned-out sofas, old shopping trolleys and smashed TVs. We made it down to about the tenth floor, and he changed direction and opened the door to the corridor – we both took a quick look and made a dash for the lift.

It was on the eighteenth floor.

Mr Baguette pushed the button, and it headed down towards us. He pulled out his gun and stood back with it raised at the door; I could feel my heart beating furiously as we waited. The doors slid open to an empty lift. Thank fuck. We jumped in and hit zero; the doors slowly closed, and we started to descend. He tucked his gun away again.

The lift doors opened on the ground floor to four girls giggling and pressing the button endlessly. We made our way quickly past them with our heads down as they walked laughing into the lift, on their way to get some coke or pills.

I followed him out the way we had come in, no stopping to sneak past the doorway; we ran, and I slipped on something disgusting and caught myself on the wall, steadying myself with the heavy bags. On we ran. We burst out of the door and legged it across the verge to the car. I could hear whistling, shouting and the buzz of mopeds. I threw the bags in the back, dived in and flung the car in reverse. We spun out of the bottom of the alley, straight into a moped that was heading towards the tower. Shit.

The driver and his bike skidded across the floor in front of the car. Mr Baguette wound down the window and fired three shots at him. He slumped over, helmet still on. I sped off and did a couple of lefts to get off the estate as quickly as possible; a couple more turns, and we'd be there. A BMW full of goons flew past us. I drove calmly on, trying desperately to control the adrenaline coursing through me; they had no idea who they were after or what had happened yet. We made it out and onto the dual carriageway. I think we got away with it.

"What now?"

"We go to Brookes Farm, you know where it is?"

"Yeah, sure, I think so, the cider place?"

"Ah yes, the apple cider you are famous for here, that is it."

Anyone would think I was taking a French friend on a tour of UK food spots, as opposed to an evening of drug-dealer hits.

I headed down the dual carriageway for another few miles and turned off just near the farm. After a few country roads, we turned onto the road I thought the farm was on. Life was hard work without the sat-nav.

"Ah, bon," he muttered. "This is it, pull over here," he said as we approached a small passing point. I pulled in as tightly as possible to keep us out of the way.

"Wait here. Ten minutes, you drive to front of house."

He disappeared into the hedges, and I looked at my

watch. It was 3.23 in the morning. I lit a cigarette and had a nosy peek in the bags. There was about forty grand in one bag and at least two hundred baggies of various madness in the other, plus a big brick of coke, maybe seven ounces or so. I zipped them back up and sat looking at my watch until it hit 3.33.

I started the car up, pulled out onto the road and headed forward; the main entrance to the farm was just ahead. I pulled in and drove to the farmhouse through the open gates and up the drive. It was a big country affair, with a small cider shop in a converted stable next door – all very fancy. There was a Porsche and two Range Rovers outside on the gravel; I pulled up next to the Porsche and kept the engine running and the lights off while I waited.

3.36, still no sign.

3.37, still no sign.

3.38, the front door opened, and Mr Baguette stepped out with a bag in one hand and his gun in the other.

He walked over and got in the car. "Allez, go, go!"

I spun the car around. We headed down the driveway at speed, my lights still off. We pulled out onto the road. Lights on, slowing down to a normal speed, trying to hold down the urge to go faster.

We turned onto the dual carriageway and made our way east.

"Is that it?" I asked him.

"Non, one more."

"Jesus," I muttered. "Where to now?"

He named a very middle-class housing development I'd driven past a few times on the outskirts of town. I turned off at the next junction and headed there. He tossed the bag in the back with the others and proceeded to repeatedly take his gun apart and put it back together. He kept a little travel grooming bag for it in his inside pocket. He spent the rest of the journey cleaning and reloading it in silence.

Ten minutes later, I pulled into the estate. There was still a sales office at the front, long since closed, with slightly aged flags waving in the breeze. I followed his directions and pulled into the visitors' car parking area, killing the engine. He screwed the silencer onto his gun and stepped out of the car.

"Wait here," he said as he closed the door.

I lit a cigarette and waited; time ticked by slower than ever, every second flicked by slower than the one before. The body count was growing by the minute, and there was at least twenty years' worth of increasingly bad things on the back seat. I'd hate to imagine what Mr Baguette would do if we got pulled over by the police. I don't think it would end well for the police. Then I'd have to go on the run with him. We'd be smuggled back to France on a small boat from Kent. We'd have to change our appearance once we got there. Hiding in France, he'd grow bored of my English ways. After two years of eating cheese and drinking wine, I'd be found with a baguette protruding from at least one of my orifices.

Fuck that.

The paranoia was overwhelming, especially since the estate was completely dead at this time of night. Every noise made me jump and sounded a hundred times louder than reality. Some foxes were trying to get in some bins over the road, and I nearly had a heart attack when they knocked one over.

I started to get the overwhelming feeling that Dave had stitched me up. He could have sent Hans to do this, or Terry. They'd both have loved it, right up their proverbial alleyways. But instead, he sends the new guy. It'll all be fine, he said. Don't worry, he said. I'll tell that to the judge, shall I? Except they know that I'm not a grass. So they probably think I'd just keep quiet and take the time. The sad thing is, I probably would. I needed this to be over. I was driving myself mad. *Hurry up, you French fucker.*

A long ten minutes and about fifteen cigarettes later, I saw a silhouetted figure limping at speed over to the car. He climbed in.

"Go, go."

I went, went!

I drove out of the estate, trying to keep to a slow speed; I had my lights on and was trying to look as normal as two men driving around a sleepy housing estate at this time of night possibly could. We pulled onto the road right behind a police car.

Fuck! Fuck!

Every instinct in me yelled out to run! I could feel their eyes burning into me from their rearview mirror. I was suddenly super conscious of every facial muscle movement. I tried to breathe and gripped the steering wheel tightly. It felt like it might snap. We drove along for two hundred yards. It could have been miles. Suddenly they indicated left at the next turn-off. Thank fuck for that!

"Follow them," he said.

"What?"

"Yes, follow them, do it now!"

I indicated left and pulled off behind them; we pulled onto the dual carriageway, keeping just below seventy. They indicated the next left.

"Follow again?"

"No, go straight."

They pulled off. We carried on.

"Bon," said the Frenchman. He certainly had some gigantic-sized balls on him.

He opened his jacket and produced a small first aid kit which he unzipped. He opened a couple of antiseptic wipes and pushed them inside his jacket. He took out some wadding and attached sticky tape all around the outside. He pushed it inside his jacket and stuck it to whatever wound he had acquired. He finished it off by wrapping a bandage all around his body and tying it off. I'd never seen such nifty first aid in a confined space before.

"Is it bad?" I asked.

"Non, just a knife. It is clean."

"OK," I said. "Where to now?"

"Now we meet Dave. We meet at the car park at back of the golf course. Dave said you'd know."

I knew where he meant; I'd been trying to set fire to its bunker not long ago. It was just around the back of the estate the warehouse was on. I headed off in that direction while he packed away his little first aid kit; he certainly came prepared. I wondered what else he had in his pockets.

I pulled off the main road and down a country lane. It was getting lighter. I swerved around a massive pothole, drove down a gravel entrance and pulled up next to Dave's car and a few others.

"Bring the bags," he said as he stepped slightly delicately out into the dewy dawn. I grabbed all the bags off the backseat. I wonder what was in bag number three. Treasure?

We made our way onto the golf course through an open gate. I could see a few figures in the light mist on the seventh green. As we walked over, all eyes turned to us.

Dave was there, and so was Terry, who unexpectedly had my friend Doris with him. There were a couple of large gentlemen with mullets who were wearing badly fitted, patchy-looking vintage suits and deer-stalkers. They must have been the New Forest lot; they got weirder every time I saw them.

We walked into the middle of the group and dumped the three bags down on the ground.

"C'est bon," said the bleeding Frenchman.

"Merci," said Dave, passing him a large rucksack full of cash.

"Mon ami." They hugged, and the Frenchman gave Dave three awkward kisses, before moving to the back of the group, his work done.

Terry came over to the bags and unzipped them. He pulled out six big bricks of cocaine and a massive lump of brown and put them into the bag of small wraps and baggies we'd got from the tower block.

He took out a few stacks of fifties and a small gold bar and put them into the bag with the tower money. He zipped the bag and stood up; he walked over to Dave and passed him the bag with the money and gold, then went to Doris and gave him the other bag with all the gear in it. Doris handed it to the older guy. He was a stocky, short chap with swept-back grey hair, a Lovejoy-style brown leather jacket and cowboy boots over denim jeans. He seemed very happy with the bag. A drunken, grandfatherly grin spread across his face. I guess there was a couple of hundred grands worth of gear in there, however you sold it. Happy days for him.

"We all good then," said Dave, holding a hand to the grinning commoner.

He held out a pudgy hand dripping with gold rings, and in a deep booming voice with an accent I couldn't quite place, replied, "Yeah, we're good. The lay-bys are all yours, and Doris here will be running this area for us now."

Doris glanced at me. He looked excited and slightly frazzled. I grinned at him. He'd done well, it had to be said. Finally, he'd be able to leave uni – he must have enough half-arsed degrees to make a couple of full ones by now.

"OK perfect, and Doris can chat to Adam if he needs anything, and vice versa," added Dave.

"Works for us," he replied.

He picked up the bag at his feet and passed it to one of the giants behind him.

"Nice to do business with you," he boomed, turning to walk back towards the Land Rover Defender that was parked next to Dave's car.

Doris followed them, giving me a quick handshake on the way past. He made a little "call me" sign as he walked off. They drove off at speed.

Terry pulled a walkie-talkie out of his pocket just after they cleared the corner.

"Stand down," he said into it twice. He picked up the bag and went over to put it in his Range Rover. I heard a crackly reply come over the walkie-talkie but couldn't make it out.

He walked over to me and gave me a handshake. "Alright, lad, how you doing? Busy fucking night with this cunt, I bet." He waved in the direction of the Frenchman.

"Yeah, mental," I said, "totally mental."

Two of the army guys who helped in the New Forest emerged from the field next to us through a hedge. They were covered in army sniper camouflage that looked like a suit made of green and brown bunting. They looked like Ali G going morris dancing. They were holding sniper rifles and had camo paint all over their faces. Good to see Dave trusted the New Forest lot then, and of course, as always, it was nice to have been kept in the loop.

I lit a cigarette and waited for Mr Baguette. He and Dave walked over to me.

"Last stop, can you take him down to the vets so they can patch him up? They're expecting you. He was just telling me you handled yourself like a pro," said Dave.

"I mostly just sat around shitting myself waiting for

him," I replied.

"You did well."

Dave and Mr Baguette embraced as only Frenchmen can with another triple kiss.

"Good to see you, my friend," Dave said.

"Merci mon ami, anytime."

We walked to the car – it felt safer now that it was over, even though I had been at multiple crime scenes tonight. At least it was pretty much only the police I had to worry about now, despite Dave's promises that they sanctioned it. I'd be glad to get this French lunatic out of the car. I still had a lingering feeling of paranoia about Dave. Was he going to stitch me up? Was I the patsy? I just couldn't work out if I was one of the gang now or if they were just lulling me into a false sense of security.

We reached the vets within about ten minutes – they were only open for emergencies until eight, so the car park was deserted.

"Do you want me to wait for you?" I asked.

"No, it is OK. I will get a taxi. Good luck, you did well tonight. Bonne journée, my friend." He passed me a wad of notes which I gladly took. Every little helped.

"Thanks. Bon journey to you too," I said and shook his leather-gloved hand. With that, he was gone from my life, onto a vet's table for a few stitches and then no doubt back to France to do God knows what to God knows who.

I headed home after picking my car up from town and dropping off this more than slightly incriminating French car. It was daytime by the time I got back. I was feeling wired and ready to explode from everything I had witnessed that night. The thought of trying to relax and get some sleep in the red bedroom from hell was not that appealing. Why the fuck did I let Dave persuade me to go with Mr Baguette? I should have just told him to fuck off. Maybe I was a soft touch, or just too polite and British to say no.

It also occurred to me in my nervous state of retrospective intelligence that very soon, I would be the only person in the UK who had been a part of the killings. It got worse the more I thought about it. The only solution was to stop thinking about it, but my brain was whirring at a million miles an hour. After a bit of digging around, I found a pack of sleeping pills. I took a quadruple dose, regretting it about an hour later as the room began to rotate slowly. I laid down and finally got some sleep.

I slept like a drugged baby for nearly twelve hours.

# CHAPTER 14

# IS THAT A HELICOPTER FOLLOWING US?

I was rudely awoken by banging on the door and my phone ringing endlessly. I looked at the screen. Twenty missed calls. It was Terry. I answered.

"About fucking time, sleeping beauty. That's me knocking; get your arse down here. I'll be in the car."

Fuck's sake. I put some clothes on, brushed my teeth and grabbed a can of coffee for both of us on the way out.

I opened the door, climbed into the passenger seat, and passed him over a can.

"Why not?" he said and cracked it open.

We sped off down the road while he explained he was just over for the rest of today and wanted to have a catch-up. Then he made sure he had my eye and raised his finger to his lips to say 'shhhhh'. I looked confused, he looked irritated and did it again.

I was only half-awake, but I figured either he'd lost his mind, or he thought we were being listened to, which also might mean he'd lost his mind. I stayed quiet and nodded.

We pulled into a small car park with a large grassy area

and a few picnic tables overlooking a river and got out. He locked up and walked over to the river, as he lit himself a cigarette and passed one to me.

"So, what's up?" I asked.

"No talking in the cars, warehouses or anywhere anymore, certainly not the phones. Someone is listening, apparently," he explained.

"When you say no talking?" I asked, not meaning it to sound like I was taking the piss.

"Don't be a twat, this is serious," he snapped at me.

"Sorry, I didn't mean it like that. What are we not meant to talk about?"

"Fair enough, sorry, a bit jumpy after last night. Just fruit talk only."

"OK, no problem."

"Mr Baguette seems to have taken care of pretty much all our problems," said Terry.

"Good old Mr Baguette," I said as I flashed back to the piles of bodies I'd seen.

"But he missed one of the younger brothers down at the tower block – the little shit was having a fag on the balcony and managed to jump down onto the floor below. He smashed his ankle doing it. It was him that raised the alarm so quickly."

"I thought it was the next customers; we saw some girls when we got out of the lift."

"No, they were just screaming and running around. Apparently, it was him."

"Little shit, where's he at now?"

"He's gone into hiding, but he's still in the area. He's

desperately trying to cling on to a bit of power, but with no family and most of their stash gone, he's pretty fucked."

"We haven't got to sort that out, too, have we?"

"No, the Forest guys have got this one. They want to stamp their authority on the area."

"Good news. I think I'm done on the killing spree front for maybe a few days," I said, stamping on my fag end. "I miss the old days when I could just sell fruit."

"Well, miss no fucking further because now all that is sorted, selling fruit is the name of the game; it's not long until the end of the main season, and we need to get some fruit sold." With that, he tossed his cigarette end into the river.

"Perfect. It'll be a nice change of pace."

We jumped back in the car and sped off towards the warehouse. We parked around the side and headed into the office. Dave, Hans and a tall, stringy guy I vaguely recognised were in there.

After the obligatory "have a nice lie in?" comments from everyone, Dave introduced me to Thomas, one of the New Forest lot. He'd been their fruit manager and was coming to work with us to help with logistics – a bit like one of those arranged marriages between a British King and the Princesses of somewhere or other back in the day.

Dave explained to us all that Terry was heading back over to the New Forest, Hans was on security and cash, I was on fruit supplies, and Thomas was on stock-up drop-offs. I think I only got the supply job because I'd slept in.

"Seeing as you like night shifts so much," Dave said

dryly.

I was dealing with the fruit unpackers, too. Dave was sick of looking at them and was just working in the side office from now on to stop him from shouting at them.

"They seem to respond best to you, fuck knows why," he said, seeming genuinely confused.

I suspect it was my lack of fruit-throwing that had swung it, but I didn't mention it.

With that, we were done. Terry said his goodbyes and headed off for another couple of weeks in the New Forest, dealing with ponies and donkeys.

I went and found a recruit from the fruit pickers to give me a hand with the evening collections. I had a cream pickup and a couple of fruit collections to do. I walked down the stairs and picked the biggest person we had working; he didn't need much persuading and, for £100, was free for the night. He was called Stan; I hadn't spoken to him before, but I'd seen him chatting to Gregg, so he'd do. Minutes later, we sped off towards a dairy farm about twenty miles away. The sat-nav took us to a lane around the back of a farm. I called the number I had, and a few seconds later, a young chap with sideburns and a substantial beard popped out of a hedge. People did that a lot around here. He was wearing blue dungarees with a dirty yellow polo shirt underneath.

He had two massive plastic containers, one in each arm, which he was struggling along with, trying to look like he could manage. I let him carry on managing and opened up the back door for him to lift them straight in.

"Thanks, you look like you need a cigarette," I offered

him one as I lit my own.

"Thanks, buddy. I'm Freddy," he said as he held out his cream-covered hand.

I shook it anyway. He had a firm handshake which went with his strong West Country accent. He was a proper farmer type.

"Good to meet you. I'm Adam."

I passed him a brown envelope; he had a quick count and seemed happy with the contents.

"That's the badger," he said.

"What's a badger?"

"That," he said, waving the envelope. "That's the badger."

"Oh, right, good, good," I remember hearing this before around these parts. I think it meant he was happy. Fucking farmers around here are as bad as the cockneys.

"Say thanks to Dave," he said as he strolled off back to the hedge from whence he came. I got Stan to check that the cream was strapped in before we set off – it would be a shame to lose a hundred litres of it all over the new van. We were off to our next collection in no time.

We chatted as I drove north – we were meeting someone just off a road near the M5. Stan was from Morocco and had hitched his way over eight years ago to stay with some of his family. He had been working for Dave every summer since then and seemed to think he was very funny.

"If you work hard, he does not throw fruit at you," he said, which seemed a very accurate appraisal of the relationship. "And I work hard, so no problem."

His logic was faultless. We pulled into the services as we got on the motorway. It was one of the new breeds of motorway services, all shiny glass and allegedly small local food brands. There was something called 'Kash N Curry' and 'Nacho Nacho Mexican', both lurking in the corner near McDonald's, along with all the other usual suspects. I headed over to McDonald's; I had a terrible nugget urge that I just couldn't shake. I walked up to one of the grimy screens and typed in twenty nuggets, asking Stan if he wanted anything,

"No, I bring food. Thank you," said Stan politely, making me feel even worse about my food choice.

I joined a slightly uncomfortable group of people mingling at the new Argos-style pickup area. As always, McDonald's was a delightful mix of healthy-looking characters, a couple of builders, a few teenagers, a family with five screaming kids, a fat bloke and a confused-looking old chap who was trying to order a tea from one of the "new-fangled" screen things and kept swearing at it.

"It keeps adding burgers," he said in frustration to a person behind the counter who looked like she'd recently lost the couple of fucks that she no longer gave.

I went over and ordered him a cup of tea, deleting the fifteen Big Macs he had added so far. I paid for it too, as he seemed a little nervous giving his card details to a killer service robot.

"Thank you so much, bloody technology. I'm useless with it." Wait 'til he tasted the dishwater tea; he'd wish he hadn't bothered.

My number was up, and I collected my nuggets and

fries, said goodbye to the old man and headed back to the van. I sat with the stereo on eating my nuggets while Stan had a much healthier-looking little pot of something stewish. Foreign muck, I think our caravanning friends would call it. I ate my American cardboard nuggets with the usual initial enthusiasm, which was rapidly replaced with a slight belly rumble and deep regret.

Thirty-five minutes later, we pulled off the motorway and onto an A road that ran alongside it for a few miles. I saw a lay-by with a lorry at the far end with its doors open and pulled up behind it. I told Stan to go and open the back doors while I talked to the driver and we both jumped out. I headed around to meet the driver at the back of his lorry.

"No Dave tonight?"

"No, mate, he's throwing fruit at the staff."

He laughed and asked for the money.

I passed him over an envelope of cash, and he had a quick flick through and seemed happy enough.

He jumped in and started passing boxes of Morrison's strawberries out to us. There were so many boxes we had to fill the front seats with them too. We crammed it all in and got out of there as quickly as possible and back to the warehouse to unload.

"Why do we pick up fruit at night?" asked Stan casually, as if it had never occurred to him that this wasn't all a hundred percent normal or legal. I wasn't going to shatter his illusion.

"I don't know, mate, just busy during the day, I guess."

"Yes, OK, very busy lorry driver, my cousin is one in

Europe, he works long hours."

"I bet he does," I said, throwing the last box of strawberries into the walk-in fridge on top of a large wobbly pile of them.

"Well, we've got one more lorry to meet tonight, so let's have a coffee and go."

"Can we smoke?"

"Yeah, of course."

"Special smoke?"

"Yeah, sure, special smoke is fine. I'll make some coffee; you make a special smoke."

I went up the stairs to the office and made a couple of coffees for us before locking up and heading out the front to meet Stan.

He was standing at the side of the car park by the van, smoking what smelt like some nice hash. I passed him a coffee, and he passed me his 'special smoke'. I had a couple of drags and passed it back.

"Does your cousin drive over to Morocco sometimes?" I asked. "As that is some proper blond Moroccan pollen. I haven't had anything like that since I was in Spain."

"Yes, Morocco, very nice. He send me a present last week. When were you in Spain?" he asked, making me wish I hadn't mentioned it. I'd tried to blank out my time there. It wasn't a memory I particularly wanted to relive. But the pollen spliff was making the memories drift back into my consciousness. I thought I'd try an honest approach.

"I was in prison there last year."

"No," he said, sounding genuinely shocked. "Prison?"

"Yes, for a bit over a year."

"Where was this?"

"Near Madrid most of the time."

"Shit. That is bad for you. My friend was in Spanish prison for two years, he say is fucking horrible."

"Yeah, that's about right. It was fucking horrible. Cockroaches. Heat. People trying to fight me because I'm English."

"Yes, they no like the English."

"The only good thing was the hash. But now I smoke it, and I think of my time there."

"I'm sorry," he said, looking sheepishly guilty about triggering my memories.

"That's OK, Stan – not your fault."

He had a few more drags, and we jumped into the van and headed off. Stan took charge of the music and found some 80s tunes.

"I love 80s music – Rick Astley, Duran Duran, is fucking good," he told me. I couldn't argue with him. 80s music had aged like a good French wine. Even Rick Astley sounded fine these days, but maybe that was just the reassuring thought in the confusing modern world that he would never give me up or let me down.

He cranked up Duran Duran's 'Hungry Like a Wolf' and we pulled out of the estate and headed towards the next stop. This one was just outside of Southampton. An hour or so later, I pulled into a lay-by with a pacing lorry driver waiting at the end of his lorry.

"You're fucking late," he said cheerily.

"Sorry, bad traffic," I lied, passing him an envelope to

cheer him up. He didn't even look in it and stuffed it straight in his pocket.

He opened the back of the lorry and told us to help ourselves.

"Can you give us a hand?"

"Sorry, I've got a bad back."

I wondered if he really did.

A couple of cars were coming toward us. I could see their lights from around the corner. I closed the door for a moment and walked around the side of the lorry out of sight. They drove past, and I could swear the back car was full of people all looking straight at me. I walked back around to the lorry doors, I don't know if it was the hash, but something didn't feel right.

"John said sorry he couldn't make it tonight," I said to him.

"No problem," he said, holding the door open.

Nobody called John did collections. Something was definitely up.

I whispered to Stan to get in the van. I think he caught my tone. I walked over to the lorry driver, put my hand in his jacket pocket, and pulled out the envelope.

"Thanks for holding that for me; sorry, I don't know where the nearest services is."

And with that, I turned on my heels, walked back to the van, jumped in and sped off. He looked confused to see us go.

"What happened, fruit no good?" asked Stan.

"Fruit no fucking good, mate, I think he was with the police."

"Fucking police," he said with a gangster enunciation of po-lease.

I drove down the road and quickly turned back onto the motorway; nobody seemed to be following us. I pulled onto the motorway and tried to blend in amongst a load of lorries. I kept checking the mirror.

Ten miles further on, and I thought maybe we'd got away with it. Must have been a stitch-up; it felt too weird not to be. Who doesn't check their money? Everyone always checks their money, and why didn't he pull me up on my made-up John?

We headed cross-country on an A road; everything was pretty quiet, and we listened to some 80s anthems and smoked cigarettes. I glanced in my rear-view mirror as I had been throughout the slightly paranoid journey. We seemed fine. There was a helicopter for a second in the distance hovering over a bridge we had just gone under. But it seemed doubtful it was for us.

We drove on for a few minutes and there it was again, in front of us and to one side, this time just hovering there.

"Look," I said to Stan.

"Helicopter."

"Yes, police helicopter."

We drove on for a few minutes with no sign of it, then it came back. I could see it hovering behind us in the left-side wing mirror. Was it following us? The helicopter peeled off over the field to the left, and we carried on for a mile or so, and there it was again, right over us. It was about a hundred feet above us and following our every move.

*Shit, shit, shit.*

Stan took some hash out of his pocket.

"What can I do with this? I can't get in police trouble," he said nervously.

"Chuck it out of the window."

He opened the window and threw it out onto the road.

The helicopter had vanished again. What was going on? Was this what Terry was talking about at our paranoid meeting by the river? Was I about to be busted for being an accomplice to Mr Baguette? Did the police know everything? Had Dave and the others been arrested already, or was it just me going down for this? The helicopter appeared again. In front of us this time, hovering by the side of the road. As we drove past, it turned and started following us. There was no mistaking it. It was definitely fucking following us. We were fucked. Or more specifically – unless Stan was dodgier than he seemed – I was fucked.

I slowed down for a roundabout. As we pulled onto it, every exit was blocked by two police cars, all with their lights flashing. I pulled to a stop in front of two police cars blocking the direction I was meant to be heading in. Nobody moved. Three policemen and a policewoman peered at us through the dark; a spotlight hit us from above. It was the helicopter again; its light poured in and illuminated us. I could see the police in the cars, looking at screens and looking at us.

Suddenly the light and helicopter vanished again. The lights in front of us went off, and the two cars backed up to let us through. One of the policemen from inside the car waved us through. What the fuck was going on?

We pulled through the two police cars and very slowly and nervously headed off down the dual carriageway.

"No police?" asked Stan.

"I don't think so."

We carried on for another ten miles, and I pulled over for a cigarette.

"That was weird," I said to Stan.

"Yes, very exciting, like a movie." I'm not sure he quite realised how close we had just been to being arrested.

We returned to the warehouse a little shaken with no fruit to unload. I wanted to call Dave, but Terry's no phones conversation was at the front of my mind. Once we'd unloaded, I dropped Stan off, thanked him, gave him a little bonus, and then headed to Dave's house. I knew which one it was; Terry had told me a few weeks before. It was (his words) "that fucking gigantic great thing near the petrol station". I buzzed the intercom at the large gothic metal front gates.

"What the fuck do you want? You know what time it is?" snarled an arsey-sounding Dave over the speaker.

"Yes, I know. Sorry. Terry said no phones, and it's pretty urgent."

"For fuck's sake," he growled as the gates creaked open.

I pulled up on his driveway. His house was a large old country mansion and was immaculate despite its obvious age. All natural stone, uplights and large pots with trees sticking out of them everywhere. Fucking fancy, I thought as I walked through the gigantic wooden front door.

"In here, you cunt," shouted a gruff-sounding Dave.

I followed his voice into the kitchen. He'd made us both a coffee and was standing next to a pristine marble island, frothing some milk. He was wearing a thick maroon dressing gown, and grown-up PJs were peeking out of the bottom. I'm not sure what I'd imagined Dave would look like at this time in the morning. I thought perhaps he slept in military fatigues or something in a light camouflage. This was all very elegant. Quite the country gent.

"So?" he said, passing me a coffee. I took a sip and explained what had happened without sounding too much like a paranoid stoner. The helicopter. The dodgy lorry driver. The police blockade on the roundabout. I left out nothing. I even told him about the 'special smoke'. Just as I finished, Mrs Dave popped her head around the corner.

"Everything OK?" she asked politely, the very picture of rural sophistication even at this time in the morning. She looked like she could pop a quick dress on and be ready for the ball.

"This is Adam, he just had a bit of an emergency at the warehouse, nearly done, love."

"Hi," I said coyly.

"Nice to meet you, Adam," said Mrs Dave. He walked over and gave her a peck on the cheek. "Go back to bed, I'll finish up here."

She went back to bed. Dave gave me a look. "Are we done then? Is that everything?"

"Yes, Dave, I think that's it. I'm sorry for disturbing

you both."

"OK, good. Well done for not talking on the phone. You are, of course, a cunt for waking me up."

"Sorry."

"We'll speak tomorrow after I've played golf with my contact," he said as he took my coffee off me, herded me towards the front door, and closed it silently behind me.

# CHAPTER 15

# BIG DOG

The next morning when I got in, Dave beckoned me up the stairs and passed me a coffee.

"So I played golf this morning with my friend."

"What did he say?"

"He had checked everything – you were right to be paranoid, but don't let that be an excuse for smoking again on a pickup."

"No, agreed."

"It was a set-up. It was the Hampshire police, they'd been looking into lorry-jacking and similar lay-by goings on. Well done for spotting it; there were cameras and old bill everywhere, ready to jump on you once you'd loaded the fruit. You took the money back and left the fruit, leaving them with nothing that would stand up in court. Total non-starter. But they caught loads of others, so they didn't give a fuck about you."

"And the helicopter?"

"Nothing to do with it."

"Fuck off. What was that then?"

"Someone had robbed a casino the night before; you two fitted the description, and the vehicle looked similar.

That's why they let you through at the end when they realised you weren't the same pair."

"Madness," I said, taking a sip of my espresso.

"Yeah, lucky break. I think you should always take Stan with you – he's a bit of a lucky charm."

"Or a curse."

"One or the other," he said with a laugh. "We're low on fruit now, Thomas has arranged for you guys to go and 'borrow' some from one of their old suppliers. He's a right cunt, apparently, and they'd been longing to rip him off for years."

"OK, I take it we're not paying."

"No, it's a freebie. It should just be sitting in an empty warehouse. Take Hans and Thomas and see what you can find."

"OK, no problem."

I finished my coffee and walked down the stairs. Hans and Thomas were out the front, smoking. We all jumped in the van.

"OK, Thomas – where are we off to then?"

"Old man Freddie's warehouse, he's a right bellend." He typed an address into the sat-nav, I pulled out, and we set off.

"Anything we need to know about this bellend then?"

"Yes, he's got a big dog, but don't worry, I've dog-sat for him a few times, and we get on a treat."

"That should be OK then."

"He's on holiday too, so nobody should be around."

"Even better."

Hans fiddled with the stereo, trying to find some

German electronic music. He settled on O.M.D's "Electricity".

"You miss the New Forrest?" I asked Thomas.

"Yes, a bit. Been there all my life, but work is work."

"Yeah, it is, still must be weird. No more ponies."

"I do miss the ponies most. It's weird only seeing them in fields."

I laughed and told him about Terry and Donald.

Forty-five minutes of idle chat later, we were getting close. I turned into a back road through some woods.

"Pull in over there," Thomas said, pointing at a little car park with some tourists milling around in it. I pulled over, and we all got out.

We followed Thomas around the corner and through some gates up a farm track.

"Once we're in, one of you can come back out and get the van."

We walked a few hundred metres up the path to a big, dirty barn. As we jumped over the gates, I heard a very loud bark. A huge hellhound came around the corner at about a hundred miles an hour, heading straight for us. Thomas walked over to him calmly.

"Hello mate, have you missed me?"

You could see the dog's attitude change mid-run – he went from attack mode to pure excitement. As Thomas knelt down, he leapt straight into his arms and started licking his face instead of the neck-ripping he'd been planning at the start of the run.

Thomas stroked him and rubbed his ear. He rolled over onto his back for a belly rub. He was a large

Doberman and Alsatian cross of some kind. Pure guard dog material.

"Don't mind him; he's a big softy."

With that assurance, we all walked over and gave him a stroke. I was glad Gregg wasn't with us.

We went around the side of the big barn to a lock-up which was humming with the electrical noise that only a big fridge can make. Thomas pulled a drill out of a bag he had with him and started drilling out the lock. We were in after a few minutes and a few drill bits. The double wooden doors opened outwards to reveal a big refrigerated room full of strawberries.

"Good," said Hans. "I get the van."

We started piling up the boxes of fruit in the courtyard. Hans pulled up a few minutes later, and we filled the van to the roof with fruit.

The big dog wouldn't leave Thomas alone and tried to get in the van with him.

"How does he treat the big chap?" I asked.

"Fucking shit, he sleeps outside in some shitty kennel and never gets any love from the fat cunt."

"Well fucking bring him then, some company for you."

He looked delighted by the idea. The dog hopped into the van without much persuasion and started slobbering on Hans. He didn't look overly happy. Thomas was alright; maybe I had the New Forest lot all wrong. They did have a bit more facial hair than everyone else, and their clothes were on the peculiar side. But if anything, Thomas seemed easier to get on with than Terry and Hans. Maybe it was the love of dogs making me biased. I always was a sucker for dogs.

Then again, isn't that how they tricked everyone into all their commoner goings on? The love of animals in England overrode a lot of negatives. That's why the Prime Minister always bought a dog the moment they got into power. The thought that we could trust one without a dog was insanity. After all, the dog wouldn't put up with anyone too awful, would they? We'd probably see them sneaking off with a knapsack on a stick if the new Prime Minister did anything too terrible.

After driving back to the warehouse and unloading at record speed, Hans and Thomas dropped me off just around the corner from mine before they both headed home.

I walked to my house to find a car pulled up in my driveway. It was a bright pink Mini 4x4. Doris jumped out of the driver's side.

"Nice wheels," I said. We shook hands and gave each other a friendly mutual back pat.

"Come in, man," I said as I unlocked the door and headed in. I made us both a coffee and skinned up a big spliff, opening the living room doors onto the garden. We smoked and drank coffee, looking at the sunny day outside.

"You good then, mate. How's the new job?"

"It's cushty, mate. No more students to deal with. Whole different thing, big-time shit."

"Any problem with the old lot?"

"Not much, the odd murmur here and there, but the

commoners are fucking on it; they fucked a couple of dudes up by trampling them with horses the other day. Honestly, they are some medieval motherfuckers when they want to be."

"Medieval mulleted motherfuckers."

We both laughed and continued to smoke.

"Did they find that last Mathews fucker?"

"No, he's totally vanished. They even put a five-grand reward out with all the local dealers for information."

"Nothing?" I asked.

"Not a sausage yet, it's like he dropped off the earth."

"What's with the wheels?"

"Oh, nothing – my car just wouldn't start, and that's my missus' car. She does mobile hairdressing."

"Clearly," I said, passing him the spliff. "I thought maybe you were branching out."

He chuckled at the thought.

"I brought you a present anyway, you sarky twat," he said, pulling a large envelope out of his bag and chucking it over to me.

"What's this for?"

"For sorting it all out, mate, wouldn't have happened without you. I'm fucking smashing it – two hundred grand in the last two days we took. It's madness."

"Well, I appreciate it, man, thanks." I went into the kitchen to make some more coffee and stuck the envelope inside a cereal box in the cupboard.

"Oh yeah, I nearly forgot. I got something for Mike too," he shouted at me from the living room.

"He'll be well happy with that, mate. He wasn't

expecting anything."

"Well, his info was priceless. They asked me to give him twenty grand to make up for that little robbery he had."

I passed Doris over another coffee, and he chucked me another wad of cash.

"You OK to give it to him? I haven't got time to go out there, and the fucker gets me so fucking high I could barely see after an hour with him last time. I had to pull over and have a quiet word with myself."

I laughed and popped the cash into a drawer. "Sure, no worries. I had a similar experience."

We sat and chatted shit about our time at uni together, selling soap bar and attending next to no lectures. Funny times. We were on different courses but managed to miss a similar number of lectures. He'd gone for the apparently easy and super useful 'Business Studies' degree, while I'd opted for the even more useful 'Media and American Cinema' option. I suppose you could argue that his current work situation was a reflection of his degree. He did seem to be doing a lot of business. I wasn't quite sure what I was aiming for when I picked mine. The only job that seemed to be even vaguely appropriate was a Barry Normanesque film reviewer, and that role had been taken by Mark Kermode of late.

"Remember that time we took acid for three days straight?" he said.

"That was madness."

"Someone drove us to the petrol station for snacks, and the guy had a squeaky voice," he recalled.

"Oh yeah, the fucking Monster Munch."

"The Monster Munch man," he said in a high-pitched helium voice. "Pickled onion, pickled onion, he wouldn't stop saying it, waving around packets of crisps. What a nutter. Weird shit happens when you trip for that long. It's like reality shifts sideways a bit, and you enter a slightly alternative reality."

"No shit. Remember that dude with the pizza who ran past us, tripped up and flew through the air and landed face-first in the open box of pizza." I said laughing.

"He looked like he'd walked off a horror film set. Melted cheese and tomato all over him, with a bit of ham hanging off his nose."

"Honestly, that shit was too funny," Doris said.

"Acid was so cheap back then, like a quid or something. Four quid for a microdot. Crazy. Those test tube trips were a lot to handle."

"The Mickey Mouses man, I loved them," he said fondly.

"I can remember coming round to yours, and you were sitting on the floor laughing and licking that big sheet of Mickey Mouses," I reminded him.

"Oh yeah, I'd forgotten about that. I done lost my fucking mind after that," said Doris.

"You were sat in the middle of the road at four in the morning, skinning up and shouting that the mouse was after you."

"He fucking was."

"Mad times, mate."

"Crazy shit."

We sat silently smoking for a few minutes. I rarely thought about my time at uni; I always figured I'd be doing something amazing all this time afterwards. I didn't know what, but I had a feeling I was destined for something great. These feelings had slowly evaporated over the years. Now, if I thought about my future, which I tried to do as little as thinking of my past, I could only see disappointment and maybe more time in prison. What a bleak change a decade or so can make; all my youthful ambition and hopes bashed out of me by life's giant hammer. I decided not to share these thoughts with Doris, who, on the whole, seemed quite upbeat about his life choices at the moment.

Doris glanced around at the house as if he had only just realised we were sitting in one.

"You renting this place then?"

"No, inherited it while I was on my Spanish holiday."

"Sorry to hear that. Anyone close?"

"Not massively, an uncle I used to get on with when I was a nipper. He didn't have anyone else close apart from a really horrible ex-wife. I think he'd have given it to anyone as long as it wasn't her."

"Well, that's sad but a bonus."

"I wish I'd hung out with him more. He was a nice chap. Always used to play computer games with me as a kid."

"Something to come back for, I guess," he said.

"Yeah, not sure where I might have ended up if this wasn't waiting for me when I got back."

"Well, glad you ended up back here, man. Sometimes

it's good to come home."

"Yeah, maybe, ask me again in a few months."

"Anyway, I've got to shoot, just wanted to come by, say hi and drop that off. I'll see you next week sometime and let me know if you need anything at all," Doris said.

"Sure, thanks, mate and good luck with the hairdressing, yeah?"

He popped some shades on and jumped into the pink car. As he pulled off, I saw that it read "Tania's Mobile Hair" on the back in big gold letters. Well, I guess he probably wasn't going to get pulled over for anything other than bad taste.

I rolled another spliff and sat back on the sofa. I was a little confused over Doris's sudden success. Even though I'd helped him get there, I couldn't help but feel that even in the criminal world, I was getting passed over while my friends succeeded. It wasn't quite the same feeling of inadequacy that I got when I bumped into someone from school who now had all the trappings of a supposedly successful life – a well-paid job, wife and kids, nice car and house – but it was definitely the distant cousin of that feeling.

A feeling deep down inside me that there was little hope of success.

# CHAPTER 16

# THE STING

The next morning I arrived at the warehouse early. I had to park around the side; there were a couple of massive white vans pulled up by the front doors. I walked in, and there were boxes and staff everywhere.

"Alright," Dave shouted over the warehouse noise. "No hanging about today, son, get stuck in. We've got a lot of fruit to get done for the last week."

I joined the mass of fruit pickers moving fruit; he had all the staff working that I'd seen throughout the summer and a couple of extras I hadn't seen before. The tables were all full of double teams; even the office upstairs had been taken over by fruit. Fuck knows why the sudden urgency, but I got stuck in. We unloaded a load of Asda strawberries from a van and plonked them on the tables in piles. The fruit unpackers ripped them open, and we loaded the new plastic-free punnets into another van.

I gave Stan a hand unpacking while his table partner had a break. He said the walk-in fridges had broken, so everyone was on double shifts today and tomorrow.

"More shifts, more money," he shrugged.

I ripped open Asda packs and poured strawberries into

punnets, loaded the punnets into cardboard trays and put them in a stack. I threw the used packs into a big black bin between my table and the next. Every few minutes, someone came along to empty all the bins. It was full-on. We loaded up the last boxes into the white van, which sped off. As soon as it was gone, a Sainsbury's lorry reversed in from where it had been waiting on the road. The driver opened the doors, and we formed a line unloading it straight into piles by the tables. He left, another two white vans turned up, and we loaded the repackaged fruit straight into the back of them.

The whole time, Dave was marching around shouting at people in between phone calls, during which he was also shouting at people. He seemed to work best in this environment. Smooth chaos, he called it; shouty madness was more like it.

After a couple of hours, twelve white vans and three lorries, Dave called Hans and me into the side office for a coffee and a break. We walked in, and he passed us both an espresso and a cigarette.

"Right, I'm off – early start tomorrow, and I need to go and drop some payments off. Can you two lock up and make sure all the fruit is unpacked and out by the end of the day?"

Before we'd even agreed, he was out of the office and giving us one of his over-the-shoulder waves.

It was eight o'clock by the time we'd finally processed the never-ending mountains of strawberries. We hosed the place down and sprayed down the surfaces. We had to do the same again tomorrow. Then that was it, just a week of pure fruit selling and none of the processing. Dave said we had enough to last us to the end of the main season.

The next day I was rudely awakened by the noise of the bin men smashing recycling bottles as loudly as they could outside my house. I often wondered if they were loud on purpose because they had to be up early, or if there was just no possible way to collect recycling without making that noise. I reluctantly got up and made a coffee before jumping in the shower. I still stank of strawberries from the day before; using strawberry shower gel was a terrible idea. I headed out of the front door and made it in before everyone else. I waited outside for everyone to show up while I had another coffee and a fag.

Dave arrived followed by Hans and then a steady stream of unpackers. By 8.30, we had about twenty people in the warehouse, and we were ready to go. A tractor with a trailer full of boxes of strawberries turned up first. Dave had abandoned all subtle collections from lay-bys and farms for the last few days and was taking a direct delivery approach.

"Alright there," said a middle-aged farmer in a thick West Country accent. "Dave around, is he?"

We pointed him up the stairs, and he waddled off in that direction.

A couple of the team jumped up into the trailer and started passing down boxes of strawberries. They weren't the cleanest, and they stunk of manure. We had to give them a little hose off before we started repacking. It was better when they came pre-packaged and wrapped in plastic. Probably not for the environment, but definitely for us. We washed them down and plonked them all over the floor at the front of the warehouse. After a few minutes, the red-faced farmer came waddling down the stairs.

"All done, are you boys?" he asked.

"Yes, mate, you're good to go."

He jumped up into his tractor and made the most enormously long-winded fuck-up of reversing back out on the road. After five minutes of terrible driving, Hans had seen enough. He pulled open the door.

"Get out; I do it," he shouted at the man over the engine noise.

The slightly embarrassed-looking farmer jumped out as instructed and Hans smoothly reversed it onto the road on his first go. He jumped out and held the door open for the farmer.

"There you go."

"Thanks, buddy. I don't normally drive this one," he said, before driving off.

A white van pulled up, and we started loading it up with boxes as quickly as possible. The fridges were still broken and the warehouse was as hot as hell. So we had to turn around the fruit as soon as possible. Dave had arranged the use of a load of walk-in fridges elsewhere. The white van pulled off, and we had a cigarette outside while we waited for the next van to arrive. A pair of white vans pulled into the courtyard in front of the gate.

"Not there, mate, pull forward," I shouted at one of the drivers. He just put his eyes down and ignored me. What a rude twat! I walked towards him to have a word.

Suddenly a couple of flashing BMWs pulled up behind them, and the back doors flew open on both vans. Police poured out onto the forecourt.

Instinctively, I turned around and legged it into the warehouse as more police cars pulled up on the road. I pushed through the throng of confused fruit unpackers, knocking a couple flying into a table as I scrambled towards the stairs. There were police in the warehouse behind me, shouting and pushing people against the wall.

Everything slowed down to a slow-motion crawl. I looked over my shoulder as I ran and could see Hans outside, up against one of the vans. I got to the bottom of the stairs and looked up. Dave was standing at the top of the stairs, calmly surveying the madness. He was sipping an espresso. The sight of him looking so relaxed stopped me in my tracks, and I just stood and stared up at him for a moment. He looked down and winked at me.

Before I had time to process it, a policeman skidded through some fruit into me and pushed me onto the steps.

"Don't fucking move," he shouted, pushing me down.

"I'm not fucking moving," I said, pushing back and trying to turn around. Another heavy-handed policewoman ran over to help him. They spun me around and pushed me up against the wall.

"You are under arrest on suspicion of employment of illegal immigrants," they started to say.

"Fuck off," I replied.

They dragged me to the front and shoved me up against the wall with Hans. I could see something moving on the roof. It was Thomas. The nutter had somehow climbed up on the roof to escape. We made eye contact; he held his finger up to his lips to not give him away, before vanishing into a tree.

A couple of the unpackers broke free from the grasp of one of the officers and made it out of the front and down the road. Three or four policemen chased after them. One of the escapees was already cuffed, he stacked it on the curb and fell on the grass. Two policemen piled onto him; the other one darted down an alley and disappeared. Hopefully, he made it.

I looked around for Gregg or Stan but couldn't see either. God knows if they were even legally in the UK – possibly not. Why else would you work for a man who threw fruit at you?

The three policemen came back with the one they'd caught and brought him into the warehouse. They were out of breath and looked flustered that they'd lost the other one. The white vans pulled back slightly as a Jag with flashing lights pulled into the front of the yard. Two men stepped out – one I kind of recognised from somewhere. He looked straight up at Dave, who was standing at the top of the stairs and gave him a little nod. The other one walked over and started talking to the head policeman. I heard him call him a "fucking idiot" a few times. Evidently, losing people wasn't a good look in the police force. The main guy walked calmly through the warehouse towards Dave, who descended the stairs.

"David Yatesbury, I am arresting you on suspicion of the employment of illegal persons."

"Fuck off, you cunt," said Dave calmly.

The whole place went silent as they came face to face at the bottom of the stairs.

"You have the right to remain silent."

"Blah blah blah, get fucking on with it," said Dave as he turned around and offered his hands for handcuffs. The sergeant, who was standing next to the head copper, put handcuffs on him, and the three of them walked back outside to the yard.

"Put those two in the cars," he said, looking over at Hans and me. They marched us over to the cars.

"Get the rest of them down the station and processed ASAP," said the head honcho to one of his underlings, "and make sure you lock the place up this time."

Hans and I were pushed unceremoniously into the back of a BMW, which reversed up and sped off out of the estate. They turned left and darted down a side road.

I looked at Hans. "Isn't the station the other way?" I asked.

"Yes, other way."

Fuck, was this a hit or something? Mr Baguette getting avenged? We pulled over on a road at the back of the estate. Fuck, fuck, fuck.

They pulled us out, and the other BMW pulled up behind us. Dave was hoisted out of the back of it. This felt like a professional hit; we were all going to die.

He looked up at me and laughed. "Don't look so fucking worried, son. They aren't about to shoot you," he said, reading my mind. "These are the real police."

Hans chuckled.

The sergeant went behind them both and unlocked the

handcuffs, then came and unlocked mine too.

The main man from earlier pulled up in his Jag behind us and got out. He was different from all the others. He had a crisp well-cut suit on and smoothed-back dark hair. He looked more like a hedge-fund manager than anyone from the police. He and Dave shook hands as if nothing had happened.

"He thought you were going to kill us all," laughed Dave, pointing over in my direction.

They both laughed. I really recognised that laugh.

"Adam," he said with familiarity, "I wouldn't kill an old school friend."

The penny dropped!

"Shaun?" I asked.

"Yes, you dozy cunt. Didn't you recognise me?"

Dave looked surprised. "You two know each other?"

"We went to school together," I said. "Sorry Shaun, you've changed a lot."

"You haven't," he laughed. "I clocked it was you the moment I stepped out of the car back at the warehouse. It's been a long time, where have you been hiding?"

"I've been about. I didn't know you joined the police."

"Perhaps if you'd stayed in touch, you might have known, you fucking idiot." I could see why Dave and him got along so well.

He flicked back into police mode. "Dave, I'll speak to you later. A pleasure, as always. By the way, I took care of those little birdies listening in on you. It was some dick up at internal affairs. All fixed now, though," he said merrily as if discussing a broken fridge.

"Adam, get my number off Dave. Let's have a drink and catch up, be good to see you."

With that, he got back into his Jag and was gone.

Dave and Hans looked at me for a second. "Pub then?" asked Dave.

"Yeah, sure, why not?" I said, feeling totally overwhelmed, and we all headed over the road to a pub a few of the team went to occasionally after work.

The whole day had been a complete head-fuck, and that was before Shaun showed up. He was one of my closest friends at school; we were in most of our classes together and hung out most days after school when we were doing our GCSEs. He was always a bit sportier than me, and I was a bit cleverer than him. I'd help him with some of his work, and he'd make me look better than I really was at football. An easy pass in front of the goal here, a not-too-suspiciously well-written essay on Henry II there.

After school, I'd been so glad to get out of there, I'd just never bothered to stay in touch. I saw him once or twice around town, but we didn't connect anymore for some reason. Now he was something fancy in the police, and he was arresting me. Funny how things turn out – not funny ha ha, more funny like a crying clown.

Dave grabbed us all a drink, and we sat in the beer garden. I felt like I was the only one who didn't know what the fuck had just happened. I took a long swig on a bottle of beer and lit a cigarette.

"Sooooo," I said, looking up at Dave for answers.

"Well," said Dave, "I'm sorry about today. Probably

should have told you before, but I wanted you to look surprised," he explained.

It turned out that most of the warehouse workers were illegal and were due to get paid for the last month's work. Dave didn't particularly want to pay their wages. If he could avoid paying something or someone, he would. He also didn't want to pay all the rent he owed on the warehouse. So every year, his golfing chum – my old school friend – arranged a little visit from the police. They raided the warehouse, took the illegals and shut down the operation. Dave would vanish, the fruit season would end, and then it would all start again the next year in a new location.

"What about Gregg and Stan?" I asked, slightly worried about my new friends. I hadn't seen them but was still worried.

"Gregg and Stan are all good, son; they've worked for us for years. We always pay them. Anyway, we need them in for the last few weeks."

"And the lay-by sellers?"

"They aren't affected – they get paid weekly, I'd never hear the end of it from those caravanning twats if they weren't."

"You'd never be able to show your face down the bingo," said Hans.

"Funny fucker. My missus would never be able to go down the local Waitrose. The wives are worse than the men."

"The wives are terrifying," said Hans as he sipped his beer.

Dave could see I looked a little perplexed by the whole thing. He told me that the landlord was a cunt, some toffy-nosed Tory twat who deserved not to get paid. He tried to explain that the police only left us alone because he helped them fulfil their quota of illegal worker arrests each year. They turned a blind eye to the rest of the fruit business just as long as they didn't have to raid endless kebab shops to hit their targets.

Dave seemed very happy with the whole thing, even though it seemed a bit on the cunty side to me. The people who needed the money the most seemed to be getting screwed over the hardest. The lay-by workers were just doing it to be able to afford new crap for their fucking caravans and holidays in the north of France. While the packers, who had to suffer Dave's temper and sporadic fruit outbursts, got utterly fucked. No money for a month of that shit and maybe deported on top of it. What a load of fucking bollocks.

"Here's the rest of your wages up to now," said Dave seeing the doubt still on my face. He threw me over a big wad of fifties in thousand bands – about £25,000, I reckoned. I popped it into my jacket and thanked him. Maybe I'd give some of this to the packers who'd been arrested. I mean, I probably wouldn't, but I should. God, I was as bad as these pricks.

"There'll be another five grand at the end of next week when we've finished all the lay-bys. We'll be working from a few different locations, so no going back to the warehouse after we've got our cars. The owner's a cunt, so we need to not show our faces, or he might want some rent," Dave added, laughing.

That must be about £45-50k that I'll be up by the end of next week, including Doris's little bonus and the money the French lunatic gave me. Not bad for some fruit selling. Probably not enough for all the other things I'd been loosely involved with, but pretty good nonetheless. More than I ever imagined that a quiet, keep-your-head-down summer job would pay.

We drank our beers, and Dave got us both another; we chatted some idle fruit chat, taking the piss out of caravans and motorhomes, laughing at the stupid tourists buying fruit and wondering where Dave could stash all the traffic-calming equipment he'd stolen over the summer for the fake traffic jams.

"Maybe you should bid on some government jobs to fix the roads; you couldn't do any worse than the cunts they normally have doing them."

"Maybe," said Dave, looking like he was genuinely considering it.

He gave me the address of places to pick up fruit tomorrow, and I said I might head back to the warehouse and grab my car if it was OK with them.

"Fine, police should be long gone by now," he said. "We might stay for a few more."

I finished my beer and headed out of the pub. There was a little alleyway leading down the warehouses over the road. I headed over, lighting a cigarette as I crossed the road. I should have had something to eat, I thought, feeling a little dizzy from the beer. I walked down the alleyway, avoiding a few dog shits.

Someone rounded the corner at the other end of the narrow path; they had a cap on and a retro tracksuit top. He was looking at the floor as he walked towards me. He walked with a limp and was manoeuvring around the dog shit as well. At the last minute, he looked up at me.

I recognised him from somewhere and instinctively said, "Alright."

His right arm flew out and hit me on the side. I jumped backwards, startled. Something in his hand flashed in the light as he hit me again – twice on the arm and once on my side. Pain and adrenaline coursed through my veins. I pushed him backwards, and he flew into the wall.

He came at me again, and I could see the blade more clearly now. I put my arms up, he slashed me and stabbed at me. I had nowhere to go. I felt the blade slip into my arm effortlessly. Then my side. Then my arm again. He stabbed and slashed.

I swung at him and knocked him back. He turned and ran down the alley, dropping the knife as he went.

He's fucking killed me!

I felt my side where he had been punching. I looked at my hand; it was covered in blood. My arms were in tatters. I staggered down the alley, my head spinning. I grabbed my phone and tried to dial the last number. It spun out of my hand onto the floor. I fell next to it. I tried to reach out for the phone. It seemed an eternity away, and I couldn't make it.

I could feel my consciousness slipping away as everything went black, and I passed out in an ever-growing pool of my own blood.

# CHAPTER 17

# THE END IS NIGH

My vision slowly came into focus as I blinked. I had the driest mouth in the world; it tasted of metal. Where the fuck was I? I looked around and saw I was in a hospital. I passed out.

I woke up again, and it was night-time. I heard someone come into the room. It hurt to move my head. A nurse appeared in my blurred field of vision.

"How are you feeling?"

I tried to speak, and it felt like dust came out. I tried again.

"Driest mouth…" I sputtered.

She passed me a glass of water with a straw. I gulped it down, it felt amazing. Water had never tasted so good.

"Thanks."

She put the glass down on the side for me and poured some more from a jug on the table.

"And how are you feeling today?"

"Blurry. What happened to me?"

"You got stabbed, your friends brought you in. You were in a right mess. Anyway, I'll leave you to sleep; just press the button if you want some food or another drink."

"OK, thanks."

I flashed back to the alleyway. Just before he hit me the first time, he looked up. I could see his face in my mind, frozen. I recognised him. He looked like his fucking brothers. It was the younger Mathews brother that had escaped Mr Baguette's evening of wrath. That explained the limp – the little fucker had jumped off the balcony to escape him.

Terry and Hans walked in with some flowers and chocolates.

"Alright, mate, you awake now?" said Terry.

"Yeah, just about. Still a bit blurry."

They came and put the flowers and chocolates down.

"Flowers," I laughed before wishing I hadn't as I coughed in pain. "It was that little fucker. The last Mathews brother, wasn't it?" I asked them both.

"Yeah, it was. We saw him come running out of the alley you'd just gone down, so we came to check you were OK."

"My fucking money!" I suddenly remembered.

"That's all fine. We got it. He was too stupid to check you for cash."

"How long have I been out for?"

"For about a week or so. You've been phasing in and out. You had about three hundred stitches in various places. Luckily he missed all your vital organs."

"What about him?" I asked.

"Your mate Doris and his commoner friends took care of him."

"OK, good."

"Alright then. We've got to get off since visiting time finished a few hours ago; we had to chuck them a few quid just to let us in."

"No worries. And thanks again for the flowers," I said with a smile.

And with that, they were both gone.

A few days later, I was well enough to get out. The fruit season had ended, and the warehouse was shut down. Dave came and dropped off my missing cash and some accident pay while I was recovering at home.

I hobbled over to the front door.

"Alright, lad, sorry, didn't mean to get you up."

"You coming in?"

"No, I won't stay; look, here's your final wages and a bonus for the stabbing. Sorry about that. I feel terrible."

"Not your fault."

"Let me know if you want more work when you're back on your feet."

"OK, thanks – I will do"

I closed the door, sat down and lit a spliff. The summer was coming to an end; I had a lot more cash than I'd ever seen before, plus a lot more stitches. I popped another couple of painkillers, had a drag on my spliff and lay back on the sofa to pass out again.

*Fucking fruit.*